PROPHECY OF A PLANET

PROPHECY OF A PLANET

ANTHONY B. SMELLIE

BOOK TITLE

PROPHECY OF A PLANET
THE MEETING
BY
ANTHONY B. SMELLIE

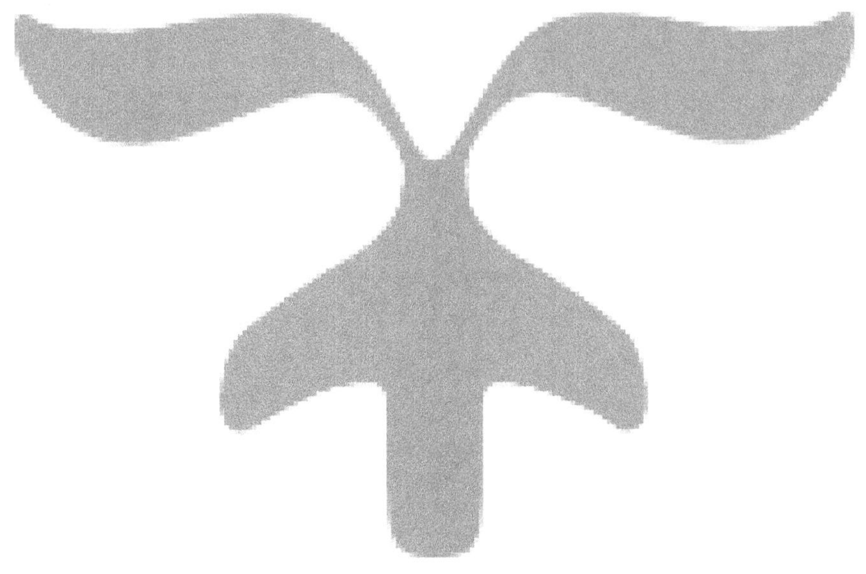

BOOK INFROMATION

This is another Diyha Promotion. Author: Anthony B. Smellie
Edited by Monica D. Dyer, and Map Illustration by Mike Yucka
Story Created in 1988, Published by Diyha Production
Soft Book ISBN- 979-8-8692-3435-3
Hard Book ISBN-979-8-8691-1788-5
eBook ISBN-979-8-8691-1788-5

******

BOOK CONTENT

******

DEDICATION

Special thanks to God, for if it were not for his blessings, none of this could have happened.
This book is dedicated to my Granny (Gwendolyn Smellie).
It was her belief in the Lord and me that kept me going. There were days when I thought I was wasting my time, and she would call me over to say, "Don't give up, you hear. Keep going for your Granny."
Thanks to her strength and her faith in the Lord, I was able to finish this novel.
Love you, Granny.
Rest in Peace
******

MAP

Jatego Range
Arkerian Low Lands
Nut River
Adean Territories
Arqua Pass
Nut River
Zannily
Land of No Life
Q~ufahti
Q~ufahti
Q~ufahti

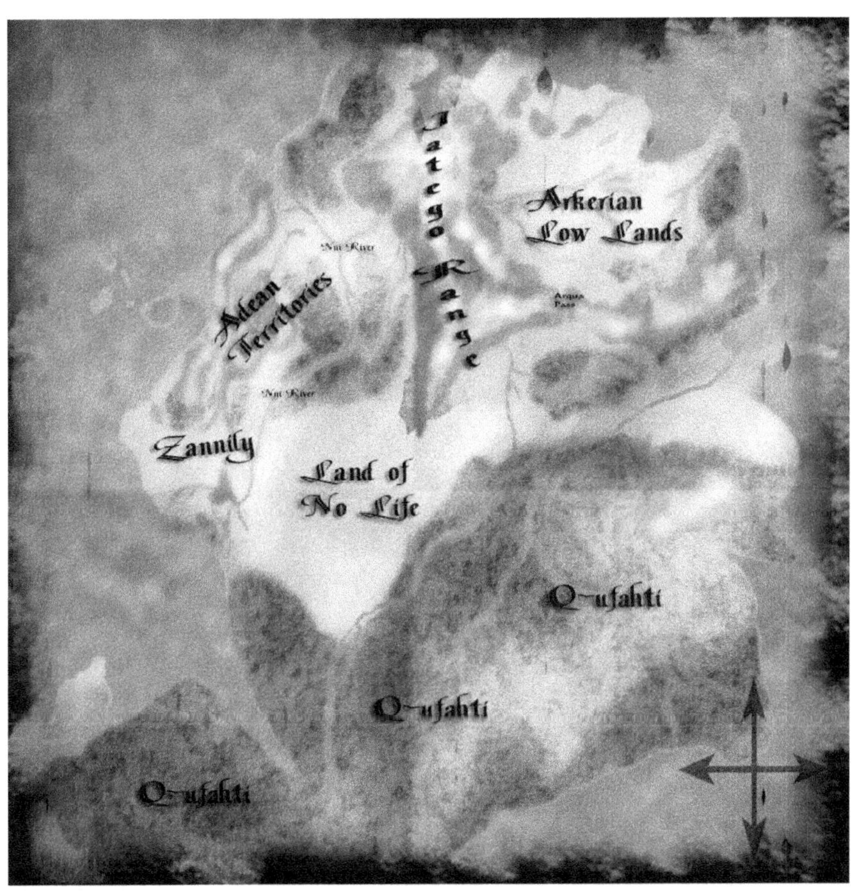

1

THE PROPHECY

A meeting will be held in a place where no one can see it. This will change everything, sending this world on a journey into Prophecy, where three arrive to sit together. They strategize a plan to set things in order.

This meeting of the minds with their plan is to defeat and conquer each of the other Clans.

When the meeting ends, they will all go their way. Each understands how the plan will work, but each has much more to say.

All three will do as their leader asks. They will send him their Ban, but distrust and deceit walk hand in hand. A messenger will arrive at the dwelling of a different Clan to tell them of the Dark Lord's plan.

But when all is said and done, a betrayer from within comes only not soon enough to stop the web from spinning or the beginning of the Dark Lord's Ambush.

******

2

PROLOGUE

**Many different Universes fill the Galaxies; each one has many different planets. In our galaxy, we have the most planets. Our story, you are about to hear, starts on the largest of these planets.

Our planet circles a large sun, along with its twin moons. Before I continue, I would like to let you know that our tongue is different from yours. With this in mind, I will explain some of our words as we continue.

We of this planet feel that the sun, which we call 'AWU' or 'Turn of the Firelight,' revolves around our planet as the twin moons do. [Because 'AWU' rises on one side of the planet and sets on the other, the inhabitants assume the sun revolves around them rather than the other way around.]

When it comes to our twin moons, we call the larger of these CHIZU', and the smaller one CHIZKA'. The light, we call 'Turn of the Twins.' As for the name of our world, it is Jahanet.

Our world has many beauties along with many dangers. One of these beauties is our tree, named Yohba. Each cycle, [year], they grow approximately twelve Ti'fin [inches], and most can reach a height of 100 U'fin [feet].

For this reason, we base the height of everything on our planet, starting from the ground up, in cycles according to the growth of the Yohba Tree.

For example, we would say that an average being on our planet stands seven cycles of the Yohba tree, which makes him or her around seven feet tall. Someone who is slightly taller, we would say, plus ten from the duration (time) of being (birth). We also measure age by the duration of cycles.

Further, we use the word 'Yohb' to measure everything in our world, such as distance and length. As for the dangers, well, one of them is the mighty Lentar, a flying creature with a wingspan that reaches one hundred cycles of the Yohba tree. The edges of those wings are as hard as rocks, and the Lentars use them with deadly force.

With these wings, they can lift a tall [adult] Dekam with very little effort. Lentars also have two tails that are as hard and sharp as swords. Like their wings, these, too, are weapons, striking freely when threatened with deadly accuracy.

Hard, razor-sharp teeth also add to their list of natural, but very dangerous weaponry. Their feet, devoid of flesh, are massive bone-like appendages strong enough to carry a full-sized being, clutched in its powerful talons. The only way to bring down one of these creatures is to stay out of its reach while striking it from underneath if you're able to do so.

The inhabitants of this world are unlike those of any of the other worlds. The main reason is that we are all born with a power linked to the core of our planet. We call this the *Dunamis Power*,' meaning *Strength from Within.'* We believe that when the Creator made this world, he made it using the power of Dunamis.

Legend has it that eons ago, the ancient beings of this planet could harness this absolute Purest, Natural, and Mystical power of Dunamis. However, over the duration, the power's influence grew so strong that they became mentally unstable.

As a result, their powers destroyed them, and the planet reabsorbed the essence of the Dunamis. Over the duration, the spirit of the cycles changed the ratio of the Dunamis into a less concentrated nature from its original power.

For this reason, all the present inhabitants who use the Dunamis, including the creatures, can harness the power, but it is only a fraction of the original essence of that power, allowing each to enhance that aspect over the duration and diligent practice. To control Dunamis's Power, we use determination, strength, and willpower.

Once we decide to do something, we can call on the Dunamis Power to do our will, and by directing/combining the power with the elements, we can build our homes, forge weapons, as well as create many other forms of energy to use at our disposal.

Although all of us can harness the Power Dunamis, only a few of us bother to use it. For this reason, those who use it are called 'Users of the Dunamis', or in a word, 'Users.'

All the beings of our world live together in what we call Clans. There are eight Clans in our world, namely, Clan Dekam, Clan Veloian, Clan Arkarian, Clan Adeian, Clan Mosaur, Clan Drehoc, Clan Ja-Ree, and Clan Trion. Many of the Clans occupy their specific geographical area known as Domains.

Four Clans live on one of the largest domains called Icka. This is a huge area that features diverse physical characteristics within its borders, such as the Q-Farhti' Forest, the Arkarian Lowlands, the Jatego high rock [mountain], the Land of No Life [desert], and the Realm [valley] of the Adeians.

There are more domains and regions that you will hear about as our story unfolds, but Icka is where our story begins. Inside one of these dwellings, one can see a big, body figure standing tall, walking around. Although all the Clans live in different domains, they all share the Icka, so they would come together to bandy [trade] with each other. They always support each other on many different adventures. Then you go to another dwelling to see a tall male dancing around, as you go to a third dwelling to see a matron walking down a flight of stairs.

All the Clans work together as one, protecting, hunting, and battling for each other if needed. For thousands of cycles, the Clans lived in harmony--until the prophecy--the beginning of 'the' battles, when one particular Adeian made a pact with the Dark-One, *that* one who wanted it all. This started the slayings of many, and the beginning of this Prophecy of a Planet.

"I grant you, all the powers of the Users along with the strength and ability of the Warrior to rule this entire Domain.

Therefore,

Your life force will not rest until the taking of this world.

Then, all will be mine."

These were the words of the Dark-One, but they meant nothing to us at first. Nevertheless, they were the clues to the unfolding of all the events that took place over the last two thousand cycles. It also led to a series of foretelling events that are now about to unfold--the prophecy over all the lands and all the Clans, that will engulf our world in many battles.

Matoca's Kazar the gates open, and a Ryder leaves the large structure on the six-legged creature. All huffs hit the ground, revealing purple dust, leaving a trail until it vanishes.

******

3

BURN KAZAR BURN

The Turn of the Twins stands strong in the heavens as a star streaks between them and the planet below. The sky is clear, and the stars can be seen from the surface of the planet, so close that it seems one can reach up and touch them.

Two beings stand on a large rock looking up into the sky. They watch as the streaking star makes its way across the heavens, but the rising smoke from a distant fire blots their vision from seeing the endpoint of the star.

Their attention shifts to the far horizon, to the reason for the smoke. They are looking at a large burning structure engulfed in flames.

The deep darkness of the Twins wraps its arms around the land as if to protect it, but the light of the fire fights to keep the Twins' inky fingers at bay, spreading over the area, illuminating the landscape like the Turn of the Firelight at the duration of dusk.

The two beings continue to watch as columns of black smoke fill the sky, giving the illusion of large, shapeless hands curling upward over their heads to touch the Twins.

The wind fills the billowing smoke with the scent of rich burning wood, mingled with the stink of burnt flesh. They are Veloians and belong to one of the clans that inhabit our world.

Waving away the smoke that blocks their view, the taller of the two watches the former great Kazar [castle], which once governed this region along with the surrounding Marluing [city], being engulfed in flames. His name is Te'Har the Na'Katon, [Leader] of his clan. He looks toward his flame [wife] Ti'Aya, he whispers.

"This is a good thing we do for the clans," but there is a tinge of doubt in his voice.

"This could be the beginning of an omen." She smiles, looking up at him.

"For our sakes, my flame, I hope not." Movement at the base of the inferno draws their attention, where thousands of beings walk away from the burning structure. Even from this distance, their silhouettes are impressive. Through the flames, the pair can instantly recognize to which of the clans they belong.

They are Arkarians, Dekams, with some Veloians from their clan. Many of the Arkarians and Dekams are already holding the reins of the six-legged creatures that they ride.

The larger of these six-legged creatures are Zaruses, and the smaller ones are Zorns. Te'Har leans slightly over the edge of the rock. His eyes pierce into the dark as the Firelight flashes across his face. Even from that distance, one can see the sadness on some of their faces.

In his heart, he knows that this is a great victory, but the cost is also terrible. The intermingled groups are slowly leaving what is left of the battlefield. Some are walking tall; some are staggering. Many carry the wounded in their arms or assist those on field-made stretchers.

This special merging of the three clans has ended. Their unity seems to evaporate, as now sadly, they separate, each clan knowing they must go their own way. The Arkarians, along with the Dekams, head toward the Jatego.

The large body mass of the Arkarians dwarfs their Dekam companions, which is noticeable even from this distance. Even as the Arkarians stop, preparing to mount their Zaruses, the Dekams begin to disappear into their underground world toward the Jatego.

Once mounted, the Arkarians head Zuroth [north] along the base of the Jatego, then Dimu [west], towards their lands beyond. As for those of his clan, Te'Har is relieved to see that they are still very strong in number as they head toward their forest home, the Mighty Q-Farhti'.

Turning towards his flame, Te'Har looks at her eyes fixed on the burning structure. She does not move, no sound; she just stands there like a statue. Her posture is like one waiting for something to happen.

With a slow wave of his hand in front of her eyes, her gaze is broken. Blinking rapidly, she turns to him. He places his hand on her shoulder, he says in a calm voice, "It is over, my flame."

With doubt in her voice, she replies. "I hope you are right. Somehow, I feel as though this is not yet over."

"Do not worry," he assures her. "It *is* over," [emphasizing *is*].

The soft glow that envelopes Ti'Aya fades. She turns to look up at him, and a pained expression washes across her face. "UH!" She gasps, grabbing her swollen midsection.

Te'Har's expression turns from relief to fear as he places his hand on top of hers, "Is the young one alright?"

"Yes," Ti'Aya answers. As quickly as it came, the pain was gone. She continues, "They are alright, my flame. One is a User, the other, a Hunter." She smiles as her strength returns. He returns the smile, bends over, and kisses her. They embrace, as she continues, "Come, our clan awaits."

He continues to smile, replying as she moves away, taking the lead. "Yes, you're right. We must go to see the clan."

With one last look at the burning structure, Te'Har turns and takes a few steps, bringing him to her side. Without another word, he takes her arm. They continue to walk away from their rock perch, leaving the flames to finish what they started.

******

4

I LIVE

The Turn of the Twins yields to the Turn of the Firelight as thousands of stars that filled the sky slowly disappear. The Firelight rising from the Dimu [West], cast its light on more of the land until finally, it shines down on the background of what looks like the main keep.

Its long shadow drapes the peaks across the valley toward the Nni Rivulet. Dawn has come, and it breaks quietly over the Icka Domain. The light reaches the center of this desolate place. The once lush, green lands have long since turned black. This poisoned land stretches Bimu [East] toward the Nni Rivulet.

Five hundred cycles have passed since the destruction of Matoca's Kazar, and that once great Marluing. The Firelight slowly moves across the area, revealing reeking green vapors, which slowly give way to the blackened land.

The land is being eaten away to expose its master--the acid lake that is its source. The creation of the lake is the result of unburied bodies along with all the Dunamis that were uttered during that duration, which has come to be known as the Great Battle between the Adeian and the Veloian Users.

{Even though other clans were also involved, it was the undertaking of the Veloians who embarked on this journey that won out in that duration.}

Inside the burnt-out structure, there are more remains. Through the damaged roof, bones bleached by the weather and picked clean by scavengers are seen. The dew from the acid lake seeps in, stripping away the remains of whatever is left. Deep inside the ruined carcass of the building, dust fills the air as the wind blows across the floor.

A faint sound emanates from under some of the rubble, a sign of life. How could this be? No one has ventured here in many cycles. Nevertheless, the signs of life are evident. A soft glow starts to seep through the cracks in the stones piled in a mound. A large stone, ever so slowly, begins to shift.

The smaller rocks on top also begin to move and roll off the mound. Underneath, there is the definite sound of a rumble. Is there a movement? Again, how can this be? However, without any doubt, a faint sound is heard. Could there be a survivor?

At this same duration, you can hear a faint disembodied voice saying the words, "Your life force will not rest..."

The voice sounds as if hovering in the wind. Slowly, under the rubble, something moves. More rocks shift once again, the wind swirls across the floor. The hollow, but distinct echo of a voice is again heard.

"Your life force will not rest..."

As the winds swirl, dust fills the air, causing more stones to roll off to the ground, which stirs up more dust. This duration it seems as if the dust has caught in its throat. Something or some being tries harder to move the rocks that have buried it.

'Where am I? What happened to me? Am I dreaming? It is so hard to move,' the being thinks, as it tries desperately to free itself, but try as it might, it seems to be quite unaware of what has happened to it.

It has not yet realized that its body has not moved in five hundred cycles. Its limbs are quite stiff from disuse, not to mention the rocks still resting on top of it.

Again, the wind moves, and again, the voice speaks, "Your life force will not rest..." Only for this duration, the being hears it.

"Hello, is anyone there?" It yells, in an attempt to get some being's attention, but no answer comes. The wind becomes still. The dust settles, and it coughs again.

Why can I not move? Why can I not open my eyes? Why does my body feel so stiff? the figure thinks, while still trying to move. *What has happened to me?*

"HELLO, ANYONE, CAN ANYONE HEAR ME?" It cries out as loudly as it can, hoping some being will come or can hear its cry for help.

However, the only reply is the sound of the wind as it blows across the floor, and an eerie voice repeating the words, **"Your life force will not rest..."**

During this duration, the voice is a lot louder. The being stops moving and listens very carefully. *'I... I know that voice,'* it thinks. Slowly, its memory begins to awaken. *'I remember something happening... I remember an explosion.'*

Confused, the figure stops moving as it concentrates on the thoughts that are flooding its mind. It takes a deep breath, exhaling slowly. Everything goes silent as it lies there trying to remember what happened. Gradually, its memory creeps back, but only in bits and pieces.

There is a long pause, then, *'I think I remember.'* The figure's brow must have wrinkled in thought as it remembers, *'I remember the pain, Dunamis Powers crashing into me.'*

Slowly, the figure begins to recall even more. *'My Kazar. They destroyed my Kazar. OH NO!* Suddenly, its memories flood in, and the horrible truth comes rushing back.

'I am buried... alive! This cannot be! I think I must have been slain.' 'The Veloians descended upon us. I felt their Dunamis burning my head. I was slain. I cannot believe I failed. I was... so close. I cannot be slain! I feel... I hurt.'

Slowly, its eyes open. It continues, *'My eyes! I can see through the cracks of these stones now. I am not slain! I live. I am buried--but not for long. The Veloians did this. They will pay greatly. I will slay them all.'*

Its eyes glow bright red, enough to illuminate the area with an eerie, crimson glow. The glow intensifies as the powerful sound of hate comes from the center of the pile like the wail of a slaying Lentar, enough to chill the blood of even the slain bodies strewn around the floor.

Without warning, there is an immense explosion. The resounding fury of the blast pulverizes the stones resting on top of the figure. Dust flies in every direction.

******

DRAKA

The Jatego is the largest high rock [mountains] on the face of the Icka Domain. It is the realm and dwelling place of Clan Dekam. It is as vast as it is high. It can take fifteen Turns of the Firelight to reach the top and twenty turns to walk around from any starting point to finish.

The realm of Clan Arkarian sits in the Bimu [East] of the Jatego known as the Arkarian-Low-Lands. It stretches across the entire width of the Jatego. This includes the Arqua Pass. From the Jatego, heading towards the Uroth [South] sits the Mighty Q-Farhti' Forest.

The immensity of the Mighty Q-Farhti' is the home of Clan Veloian. It stretches as far as the eye can see. It would take approximately twenty turns of the Firelight to cross this territory, in any direction. It goes all the way towards the great waters, which takes ten more turns of the Firelight to reach.

Heading towards the Miu [West] from the Q-Farhti Forest, a narrow path goes all the way to the Land-of-no-Life [desert]. From the edge of the forest, across the Land-of-no-Life, it takes five turns of the Firelight to reach the Caves-of-Fulclin.

Going Zuroth [North] from the Caves-of-Fulclin sits the realm of Clan Adeian, called Zannella. It is one of the largest Adeian Marluings

[city] in this domain. Its location is exactly on the other side of a few more high rocks [mountain range].

From the Caves-of-Fulclin, it takes sixteen Turns of the Firelight to reach Zannella, but one would have to cross the high rocks to reach it. To go around, it would take thirty-two turns of the Firelight.

A swift wind blows across the top of the Yohba Trees as they spread their branches high in the sky. The graceful movement gives the appearance of dancing. At ground level, the grass yields to the force of the wind.

In some areas, the grass reaches the height of a tall Adeian. Off in the distance, a large, winged creature flies over the valley below, vanishing in the far-off horizon.

The valley itself is rather large. The Nni Rivulet [river] that flows through it stretches as far as the eye can see. It is the main water supply for Icka, but it has been many cycles since any of the inhabitants of this world ventured into this region of Icka.

Over the cycles since the Great Battle, the scorched land has tried to reclaim what it lost to the acid lake. However, the battle is lost before it begins, due to the complexity of the lake's essence.

The only sign of life in the heart of this valley now comes from far beyond the blackened ground of the acid lake, which surrounds this ominous structure.

It has been many cycles since that explosion inside the Kazar. Two large black pillars have grown out of the main keep that appear like horns ripping through the sides of the walls.

Their threatening presence as they reach up toward the heavens gives the impression of sentinels watching over the Kazar—untouchable--silent watchers of the land.

They were created when the Great Utterances caused stones from a pathway to pile on top of each other. It now shares the fate of the collapsed keep and its outlying buildings.

For more than one thousand five hundred cycles since the battle with the Veloians, not one being has ventured this way. Off on the distant horizon, a lone rider on a six-legged creature travels on what was once a path, toward the structure.

The rider stops at the top of the low rocks [hill] overlooking the overgrown path. He is an Adeian by birth. However, to look at him, one would think otherwise.

Sitting tall on the creature, he surveys the landscape, and what he sees reminds him of the way it used to look. He studies the structure and notices that the walls reveal something more. Black claw-like objects extend out, then back into the walls, almost as if a Lentar had its talons wrapped around the keep itself.

The wind changes direction, even after all these many cycles, the stench of those slain is still evident in the air. At one point, the toxic reek from the remains of the bodies was so potent that the smell was enough to render a being unconscious.

The rider remembers the battle, which took place here cycles ago. He is still finding it hard to believe the destruction that took place here in the last two thousand cycles.

He remembered how all the clans came together; how the Veloian Users rendered their utterances which started the fires. Because of that battle, the structure has become a blight on the face of Icka, and a scar on Jahanct.

He could not believe that so many cycles ago, this structure had dazzled the region with its awesome life.

He remembers the duration when many came from all over to bandy [trade] within its walls, he remembers vividly, the Marluing growing because Adeians of all classes wanted to come to live here.

What has brought this dramatic structure, once known as Lord Matoca's Kazar, to this--a pile of rubble and debris--nothing but a burial ground for the slain?

At first glance, the Kazar looks like two twisted shapes of vines and rocks built as one, and it is as black as the Twins when they are in hiding.

It is hard to believe that this structure once governed this region. This was the only Kazar in the entire domain at that duration. Now, the Kazar in Zannella governs this region.

The question in this rider's mind is, '*What has happened to Matoca, and why has he changed so drastically?*' That thought comes to him as he slowly dismounts, walking his creature down the path toward what used to be the largest Marluing under the single rule of one Adeian, Lord Matoca.

All this is now sitting under a lake of acid, which surrounds the Kazar like some kind of protective water defense. He remembers Scarra telling him that the lake formed after the battle with the Veloian Users.

He also remembers her saying how the Veloians' Dunamis were so great, that it caused the ground to spew up caustic water all around the Kazar.

As for the lifeless land, well, she said, it stretched around the lake in a complete circle, ending only four or five Yohbs short of the Nni Rivulet. '*Funny,*' he thinks, '*he could never figure out why it did not reach the Nni.*' He stops in the meadow near a tree. Absently, he strokes the mane of his Zarus, talking softly.

"Well, Torian, it looks like we are back again. I know thou hast never been here before, but your sires before you have. You are my third Torian to have journeyed here with me." He reaches into a pouch lying over the creature's back and pulls out something to eat.

Releasing Torian to graze on some of the tall grass nearby, he takes a deep breath, trying to recover from his hard journey. He sits down among the meadow plants and leans up against a young Yohba tree.

While staring at the Kazar, he starts humming a tune to himself, which is unusual especially for him, because he is not the singing kind. To look at him, one would never think he has any warmth within. However, it is not so, for there is one who knew his warm side, she was the only one capable of reaching it.

The reality is, if it were not for her, he probably would still be under Matoca's control. She was the only one who could bring a smile to his face. She brought many things into his life, music is one of them.

The song he is humming now is a popular one throughout all the Marluings. However, only the young ones sing it now. Still looking in the direction of the Kazar, the words begin to form in his mind a soft ballad issues from his lips.

"THE MIGHTY ONE, MATOCA, ASCENDS WITH POWERS RECEIVED FROM WHERE ILL WILL BENDS AND THE NOBLE LORDS ROSE TO DEFEND."

'Noble Lords, what a jest,' he sighs. *'I know all of his nobles, or maybe I should say, I know the Adeians he made nobles. What a jest,'* he repeats. Turning to Torian, he continues out loud.

"Would you believe he made *me* a lord as well? I think he did it because he thought I might slay him while he slept. The truth is, I could care less about him or the other lords. All I wanted was some land and to be left alone. So why am I here?" He pauses for a long duration before he takes his next bite from a piece of bread.

He drinks something out of a sack made from the hide of a Rookile, a dangerous creature that lives deep in the wetlands. Almost reluctantly, as if compelled, he turns his attention back to the Kazar, staring at it for a few durations. Again, he pauses a while before finishing his meal. He wipes his lips, musing. Finally, he says.

"Maybe I need to know what happened." He pauses, shaking his head, then continues, "Maybe I need to know where he has been all these cycles. Maybe I do not care. I just do not know."

Stopping thoughtfully as he raises the sack to his mouth, he takes another mouthful of the liquid and continues.

"The Mighty Matoca ascends," he shudders. "Well, Torian, enjoy this bit of good food, it might be the last you will get for a while. We do not know what kind of food, if any, we will find in there." Leaning back against the tree, his attention shifts to watching Torian as she grazes.

Looking at her, he starts thinking about all Zaruses, and how faithful and gentle they can be to their master's once they have gained their trust. However, do not take them lightly, for if mistreated, their hooves can rip a hole in the chest of any Adeian, no matter how tall.

He watches Torian with great interest and respect, his faithful Zarus. Like all Zaruses, she is an extraordinary creature. From the ground to the top of her head, she stands seven cycles of the Yohba tree, some even grow to the height of eight Yohbs.

Her six legs give her an advantage on the battlefield. He looks at each section of her legs, something he has done several durations before. His eyes shift to her hind legs, the most powerful part of her body. They give her a powerful kick-off when on a straight run.

This helps the Zaruses with speed for riding into battle or chasing some being. It allows all of them to travel up to three-hundred-sixty steps per span [one thousand five hundred miles-per-hour].

The width between her two sturdy hind legs allows the Zarus to have a steady stance, which helps when it comes to carrying things, as well as their owners.

He looks at her main legs. The ones in the middle are used for balancing during the run and provide stamina for standing, especially while in battle. As for the front legs, they are used for close battles, as well as speed.

His eyes move towards her hoofs, which, unlike the other four legs, the front ones have toes, three on each foot. The toes move independently of each other. While running, they grip the ground, which helps with their speed, which is unmatched. It also gives them the ability to change directions suddenly.

His eyes finally rested on her most important part, her head. Looking at it, he cannot believe the size. If it were not for her thick neck, her head would drop off her body. He stops for a moment, chuckling slightly.

It does not surprise him that she can see so well because of the position of her eyes. She has three of them, one on either side of the head, plus one in the middle.

'I guess this gives them the ability to see in all directions at once,' he thinks, continuing to smile. As he sits there staring at Torian, his attention moves to her coat. Except for the irregular white streaks on her snout and flank, her coat is as black as the Turn of the Twins when they are hiding.

Almost as dense as the black Kazar in the distance, the armor he had made for her covered her from head to hooves. On her sides hang his battle ax and buckler-weapons forged and used with deadly precision.

As for her master, he is well known throughout his clan as Draka. His skill is also well-known by all and feared by many. An Adeian at his duration of being [birth], to look at him, one would judge him to be an Arkarian. His height alone is one Yohb higher than the tallest Adeian.

His skin is also darker than most Adeians, and his enormously broader frame dwarfs the young Yohba tree he sits under. This is the reason many within Clan Adeian believe him to be Arkarian-born.

However, very few dare to question his heritage in his presence. Because he is an incredible warrior, but his temper is even more legendary. Draka sits back and surveys his surroundings.

He remembers the first duration they brought him to this domain, the region known as Matoca's Realm. He remembers how he was treated as a bondservant from the Outer-Regions, *{**The Outer-Regions are remote areas, smaller than even a tiny village**}*. His mind wanders back to all that had happened to him when he was a young one [child].

'I hated being born into a clan that treated their own like they did not belong. If it were not for Scarra, who found me and treated me with kindness,' he paused for a moment, *'I am not sure what I would have become.*

She made the others treat me differently. She made them wash me, feed me, and teach me the way of the sword. 'In one way, I was like her favorite. Her younger one, Yar, did not see me like that.

He saw me as one who came to steal her away. She had always been up-right with me, maybe that is the reason Yar hated me and still does. Maybe it was because his Sire looked at me with sympathy. I do not know.

'Yar was such a fool, always trying to show her how much better he was with things. He always wanted to be better than me, even though he is a much better User than I could ever be. Maybe that was the reason I took to the sword so well, like the Arkarians.

Maybe that was the reason Yar keeps calling me a half-breed. I do not like being called that. It makes my blood boil, and he knows this. Scarra kept telling me not to let my anger show; that it will let Yar know it gets to me. I tried to control it, but he just kept pushing until I...'

Draka grabs his sword as if ready to go into battle. He stops, takes a deep breath to calm himself, then returns to his musings.

'Enough of this,' he thinks, 'I really must learn to control my anger.' Pulling himself together, he looks at Torian as she digs into the ground. His gaze shifts back to what was once a Kazar of influence.

'How could this have happened? The mighty Matoca ascends. What a jest. I remember the first duration I saw him. He never treated me as if I were an Adeian. I could not remember him speaking directly to me.

If he did, it was always through Scarra. He was so sure he would rule this region. What I want to know is, how did he get to be so strong? The Matoca I knew was never strong enough to battle one Veloian User, much less take on a Clan. However, he took on three of them.

How did he do that? On that Turn of the Firelight, he fought like someone I had never seen before. The way the Veloians fought that same duration makes me think that somehow, they knew what he was up to. The question is, how?'

Draka's eyes move across the land from left to right, then it stops. Slowly, his eyes move back across the land. He realizes that there is a one-acre area that is cleared just after the blackened ground.

But how? The rocks and trees seem to have moved somehow. *'What is he up to now?'* Draka thinks, shaking his head and wondering again why he is here. He shifts his gaze toward Torian and then says.

"Okay, Matoca is up to something. During this duration, I want to know what it can be." He turns his head and looks at the Kazar again, as he continues to say out loud, "What are you up to, Matoca?"

Draka is one of three Adeians who is about to--once again--change the course of history in this Domain of Icka. He studies the land again while singing in a low voice, the song that seems to haunt him.

THE MIGHTY ONE, MATOCA, ASCENDS WITH POWERS RE-CEIVED FROM WHERE ILL WILL BENDS...

"Where did he get his powers? I know he had powers, but it was not as strong as that turn of the battle with the Veloians," Draka continues speaking to himself. There is a movement. His attention shifts from the Kazar as the light of the Twins reveals another Zarus.

The Zarus and their rider come slowly down from the Jatego high-rock range and head toward the Kazar. With a steady gaze, he can recognize the rider on the Zarus as Scarra. His curiosity peaks.

*'Why is **she** here? I thought this meeting was going to be the Lord's.' What kind of meeting is Matoca having to invite her?'* Standing up, he throws away what is left of the food he is eating.

He looks at Torian while saying, "This meeting looks like it is going to be a good one." He begins to laugh at himself when, out of the corner of his eye, he spots another Zarus heading toward the Kazar.

He turns his head quickly, and focuses to see if he recognizes this rider, he does. His eyes close ever so slowly that it seems as if he is squinting.

With a deep breath of disgust, involuntarily, the name of the rider escapes his lips. "YAR." His hands grip the air as if he is choking the life out of some being, "That mistaken Life Force of an Adeian. The last duration we met, my sword thirsted for his blood." Bitterly, he growls as he pats Torian on the neck,

"This is amusing, Torian, for my sword always thirsts for his blood, and one of these cycles it will get it. This meeting better not be a waste of my span {hour}." Grabbing Torian's reins, he mounts quickly and rides down the low rocks towards the bridge leading to the Kazar, trying to get there ahead of Yar.

Crossing the bridge, he reaches the gates where he stops, waiting. He watches Yar's approach with great interest. His mind goes back to the first duration he met his flame, Tri'Ela. It was in the bazaar; at the Marluing we now call Zannella.

He had gone there with Scarra, who was looking for some herbs she needed for her Sire, to make a drink to help him with his wounds. Her knowledge of herbs would help him heal faster.

******

6

THE BAZAAR

"D raka," Scarra had said then. "Wait for me over by that weapons cart. I will be there after I get what I need." Draka nodded in obedience. She smiled at him and walked toward the herb shop. He smiled back and then watched as she walked away.

Turning, he was making his way toward the weapons cart when he saw her. Tri'Ela was standing across the busy bazaar with a few of her companions. At that same duration, she looked across the bazaar and saw him looking at her as if she were a quarry.

Their eyes met. She smiled at him, and he returned the smile. 'Her statue is like a Queen,' he thought. He turned away from the weapons cart, and his steps took him on a direct path towards Tri'Ela. When, without warning, Yar appeared in front of him with a smirk on his lips and mischief in his eyes. He looked at Draka and said,

"What brings you out here amongst us? Could it be that you can act like us? Maybe you think you are one of us. Or could it be that you are like the mighty Lentar, who feels like they own the sky?" Yar asked, waving his arms in the air, imitating the flight of a Lentar.

He continued. "Think about this, I was in the bazaar looking for something for some being when I turned the corner, and to my surprise, you are here. At first, I thought I was seeing things. So, I rubbed my eyes to look again.

Then I said to myself, 'Yes, it is you.' That is when I saw you crossing over. It looked as if you were in a hurry. So, I had to come over to see why you are walking so fast."

The lanky Adeian moved from side to side in front of Draka, being an irritant. He stood at the height of Draka's shoulder and acted as though he could squash Draka with a single thought.

"Yar, this is not the duration. I do not wish to talk with you," Draka said, walking around him. Yar stopped for a moment, then thought. *'What is this half-breed talking about? This is strange, very strange, even for the half-breed. He did not swing at me. Why? Something is not right. Something or someone has his attention. But what? Who?'*

Yar looked around the bazaar. Then he looked in the direction Draka was heading. Again, mischief sprang up in his eyes as he saw what had Draka's attention. Yar made a step forward instantly, he shifted: {**This is the ability to move between planes.**}, and reappeared in front of Draka again, saying,

"Why the big mystery, my tall, stalwart friend? Could it be that matron across the way?" Yar leaned in toward Draka while pointing in Tri'Ela's direction.

Draka stopped in his tracks looked at Yar then said, "I am not here for your amusement Yar." He then sidestepped to Yar's right and headed straight for his target, Tri'Ela.

'I hate it when Yar and the other Users utter their Dunamis. It never impressed me. I cannot understand why I like Scarra, and she is a User', Draka thought to himself as he continued to step around Yar.

'He knows I hate it when he uses his powers because it never impressed me. Besides, Yar is more like a trickster than a true User. How could any Adeian value him?'

Stopping, Yar waved his hand and then vanished, only to reappear in front of a cart just to Draka's right.

"Are you going over to see that matron? If it were me, what I would do is dress a little better. I think if I were going to see a matron like her, I would at least wash."

He made a funny face as if smelling something offensive, then continued, "I had the opportunity to take in your scent when I leaned into you, I have to say, the smell..."

He waved his hand in front of his face, then continued. "Yes, I think you should wash, especially if you are going to talk to her. Come to think of it, I think you are going to make a fool of yourself, half-breed," Yar sneered.

Without blinking, Draka's sword swung through the air toward Yar's neck. However, Yar was waiting for this; the only thing the blade cut was the air left by Yar as he quickly shifted. The force of Draka's sword swinging through the air sang as he attempted to cut down an imaginary foe.

"AAAAGH!" Draka screamed, turning over the cart he stood near, as he continued screaming. "YAR, SHOW YOURSELF TO ME, SO I MAY SLICE YOU UP AND FEED YOUR CARCASS TO THE ROOKILES."

He looked up into the air as if searching for something else to cut down.

"YARRR," he yelled out once more. His knees and body bent slightly over, like a Leonine. *{**A cat-like creature that lives in small groups.**}* He turns around, still looking for Yar.

Realizing he was not going to show himself, Draka then straightened up, took a deep breath, and sheathed his sword. He turned and then walked off, thinking about what Yar had said.

"That Adeian wastes the air by just breathing," he fumed. He looked around as if Yar was going to show up again to vex him some more, when out of the corner of his eye, he saw Tri'Ela smiling at him.

'Is she smiling at me, or because of what I did?' he was not sure. One thing he is sure of is that smile. It had been over a thousand cycles since her slaying. The thought of her smile still warms his heart.

"Draka, Draka." He heard from his left. Turning, he saw Scarra walking out of the healers' hut, coming towards him.

******

7

YAR REMEMBERS

"Draka, Draka." Again, he hears his name as he did then. He shakes his head, coming out of his reverie. He looks in the direction of the sound. He can see inside the courtyard, along with the other two Ryders, and he is about to join. Draka rides into the courtyard.

Yar watches with interest because the voice Draka hears is Scarra's. *'She seems to be happy to see me, or is she?'* Draka thinks as he rides past Yar, whose attention is trained on Scarra as she watches Draka riding up.

'I cannot believe what I am seeing,' Yar thinks to himself as he studies her closely. *'Her eyes teared up for him. How could she tear for him and not for me, her young one? How could she look at him with so much compassion?'*

Yar continues to stare at his Sire and remembers when he first met Draka.

******

I remember when Scarra first brought him into our dwelling as a bondservant. I would watch as she went out of her way to make him feel like he belonged, as if he was born here. I remember her telling me that Draka does not have a Sire as I did.

What I also noticed was that Draka did not have to try very hard to get her to notice him. I did what I could to make him feel welcome. I tried to be *"kind"* to him, and I remember how he rejected me.

I remember walking up to him, asking very politely. Are you an Adeian or Arkarian? You have the face of an Adeian but the build of an Arkarian, so which one are you?"

Yar remembered waiting for an answer, but none came. That was the first duration that Draka heard Yar say those words, which pushed him to the point of rage. Yar looked Draka in the eyes and then said.

"Well then, since you have no tongue and I do not know what to call you, then you will now be known as the half-breed." Yar's lips curled in spite. "I hope you like your new name."

Draka looked at him and said quietly, "Do not call me that."

Smiling, Yar said in a sarcastic tone. "By the High-One, the half-breed can speak."

"I asked you not to call me that." Draka, being taller than Yar, looked down at him as he spoke. Yar looked up at him and then replied.

"What is the matter, you do not like the name? Well, I do not care. From now on you will be known as HALF-BREED to me! HUH!" Yar sneered. That was the first duration Yar felt Draka's fist across his face. His body went flying across the room only to be stopped by the wall.

Getting up on shaky legs, Yar leaned up against the wall for support. He tried to point at Draka, but his unsteady hand shifted to the right and then to the left. After half a-half-of-span, Yar caught his breath, saying,

"You are lucky my Sire is in the other room, and I have to treat you like a kinsman [brother]. That is my Sire's idea, not mine. Now I have to go and practice my Dunamis." Yar started to walk away, but then he stopped and turned back to Draka.

He continued softly, "There will be a turn when she will not be around. Next duration, you will not catch me off guard. This I promise." He turned and walked out of the room on unsteady legs, wiping the blood that was streaking down his face.

******

Yar shakes his head to get out of his trance. He always had a strong dislike for Draka. He can never quite understand why he has so much hostility toward him.

Maybe it is the way he and Scarra are so close. His gaze shifts back to Draka as he rushes towards them. Quickly, he turns and glances back at Scarra.

He watches her eyes as they slowly turn to sadness.

'I cannot believe this, the sadness I see in her eyes. It is strong like the kind one has for one's young one. How can she have such passion for one such as him, while as her first-born, I have to beg just to get her to look my way?

What do I not understand is, how can she look at that half-breed with so much flame? I remember spending much duration trying to show her, my Sire, how good I was, but whenever Draka is around, I seem to vanish into the background.'

The thought of it all sickens him. Unable to bear it any longer, he looks away. Even though Yar is a lord, his slimy countenance places him more along the lines of a Sana, {**A creature that crawls on its belly, waiting in the marsh to strike at his victim**}.*

Yar's eyes quickly flash as he looks in Draka's direction. He says loudly,

"Oh look, it's the half-breed." His eyes continue to glow. Draka noticed the light in Yar's eyes. He never trusted Yar at any rate, but he is also wary never to underestimate him.

Scarra turns to him, slightly shaking her head and saying. "You know he does not like it when you call him that."

She smiles at Yar as she comes out of her previous thoughts of Draka.

"I do not care what he likes," Yar replies rudely.

Scarra dismounts from her Zarus, replying, "I do not believe you forgot what happened the first duration you both met." She begins to straighten her clothing. After that, she starts searching through her bag. Pulling out a brush, she proceeds to tidy herself up after her long journey.

Thinking back, Yar knows that he had always been a trickster. He never felt it was his fault if some Adeians were slain while he was playing his tricks. After all, even the best Users can make a mistake. On the other hand, Draka is one he does not mind playing his tricks on.

Yar's eyes glow brightly as a disgusted look comes over his face. He continues to look in Draka's direction, in a low voice, he says to her in answer to her earlier question.

"That last duration, he caught me by surprise. I assure you that it will not happen again." The strange thing is that Draka is always catching him by surprise.

Walking past him, Scarra looks out of the corner of her eye, shaking her head, whispering, "You will never learn."

A tear rolls down her cheek, knowing in her heart that they will have nothing to do with each other.

She thinks, *'One of the reasons is that Draka does not believe in Dunamis. The other reason is that he hates Users; he wants nothing to do with them. I think there is more to it, but he is not speaking, and I will not push him.*

He believes it is not an honorable way to do battle. Somehow, I think Yar has something to do with his feeling this way. Yet, he does not mind being around me.' For some duration, she regrets bringing him into the fold.

Yar's thin brown face scowls as he focuses on Draka. He whispers.

"There will come a duration, my companion, when I get the upper hand." His eyes narrow slowly as he continues staring at Draka.

Draka looks around, and for the first duration, he remembers all the Adeians who were slain on that turn. He remembers the sound of many Zaruses riding into the courtyard, many of them carrying Arkarians.

The Ban rode hard into the courtyard trying to confuse them; it worked. He remembers the ringing sounds of swords clashing. The screams of Adeians as Arkarian swords slashed their bodies.

If it were not for Matoca and his Users who gave us the upper hand; at least that is what I thought, then. It was not until I saw the rest of the Bans. That was the first duration I saw all the clans coming together to battle us. Many Adeians were slain on that turn.

Draka looks up into the sky. The face of his flame flashes into his mind. His eyes shift to an object to his left as he passes it. At first glance, he thinks it to be a statue. It turns out to be thick vines growing out of the muck of the slain, showing bits of bones in its tendrils, steeped in the atmosphere.

Scarra stops brushing her hair and then turns in Draka's direction. She remembers [when Draka and Yar were younger], watching them bicker, how they worked off each other. She remembers how much she enjoyed both of their company for different reasons.

She starts to reminisce but fights back the urge. *'Now is not the duration for reminiscing,'* she thinks, as she looks up at the Kazar. Her thoughts dwell on Matoca, why after all this duration, he has called them.

'Where has he been? Why has he returned? Why has he called this meeting? What of the others?' She has many questions, but she is patient. The answers will come to her one way or the other. All she has to do is wait. Her eyes flash quickly and then dim.

Draka, seeing this, pauses for a moment. He stops Torian, his hand on his sword. Slowly, he checks to make sure everything is all right before dismounting. It has been many durations since he has seen Scarra. He is not sure if she has changed.

'There is one way I can tell if she is still the same. If she smiles when I look at her, she is good, but if she does not, their body will join those who are long gone.'

His mind continues the thought as he dismounts and walks between them. Draka glances toward Scarra and nods his head slightly, without glancing in Yar's direction. He continues to pass them, studying Scarra, who smiles. As he goes by, his hand slides off his sword.

She falls in behind him, leaving Yar to bring up the rear. While Draka makes his way toward the Kazar doors, he makes a cursory survey of their defenses. As he glances up at the battlements, he observes, *'He has Wards posted everywhere.'*

He smiles to himself while continuing his thoughts. *'Not bad, Matoca. This will make scaling nigh impossible'*, shaking his head in appreciation of what he sees.

*'Yes, not bad at all, Matoca. You are finally using your head instead of that Dunamis Power. This is a very good tactical move. For any being to infiltrate this relatively recently created **"island,"** they would have to cross that new bridge. The acid-filled pond has destroyed the Marluing.'*

Before he walks into the Kazar, he turns to look back at the bridge, thinking, *'The bridge itself is wide enough for five Arkarians to ride across abreast. Once they crossed, they would have to ride down this road leading to the Kazar, not to mention this massive new gate and walls. Getting through them would be a mission.*

Oh yeah, I forgot about the thirty Wards stationed at the bridge by the main gate. What a jest! Did he not learn from the last battle? Five Arkarians would ride through them as easily as water flows out of your hand. He has something else up his sleeve. The question is what?'

Laughing to himself, his thoughts continue.

'Matoca must be afraid of something. What is it? It could not be the Arkarians,' counting them off. *'They have no more need to battle anyone. The Veloians have been quiet for several cycles now.*

They do not even know he lives; for if Te'Har knew Matoca was alive, he would not hesitate to send his clan back into battle. Only this duration, the Veloians would make sure Matoca is slain, including all with him.

'If this is not his worry, then something else must be bothering him, but what? Who is he afraid of? It is not like him to hide in the shadows. Maybe Matoca was so badly beaten he had to retreat!'

He takes another look at the Wards along the walls. His thoughts continue. *'These Wards are different from the ones I am used to seeing.'*

He watches them closely for a while. It seems as if some of their bodies completely disappear from view. Captivated by the idea, he explores that thought a little more.

'They are the same height as the average Adeian, but these are clad in something different. It makes their clothes seem to shift, disguising their true forms. How could this be? How did Matoca come up with whatever this is? These must be the Dark Ryders Matoca mentioned before.'

He takes a closer look as he walks past one of them. *'They seem to be wearing hoods or masks that shift when they move. Who are they? Where did they come from? What are Matoca's plans for us all? Maybe this meeting will answer my questions.*

As he walks into the entrance of the Kazar, he remembers the last duration he saw Matoca. It was during the Turn of the Firelight when the Veloian Users battled us.

It reminded him of the destruction of the Kazar. He remembers that well because of the scar he received while he and the others barely escaped with their lives. His reminiscing takes him back to that Turn of the Firelight.

✳ ✳ ✳ ✳ ✳ ✳

8

BATTLING CLANS

The gate of the Kazar grounds burst open from the powers of the Veloian Users. The Arkarians were the first to enter. At the sound of their warriors' cries, many of Matoca's Wards ran. As for the rest, the Arkarians' swords quickly cut them down.

What caught us all by surprise was the Dekams. They came running in from behind, making their way under the Arkarians' Zaruses. They moved with such speed that the Wards were unable to strike them. That is when the Arkarians' blades struck through the Adeian Wards.

The slaying of many came quickly and painlessly. What the Arkarians missed, the Veloian Hunters did not. This was not the first duration I saw the Veloians in action, but I forgot that they were so fast. Their movements were graceful and fatal. It was like watching them dance.

Even as I struck down a few Arkarians, I could not keep my eyes off the Veloians. Their movements attracted me. It was flawless the way they would run, jump on, and off the shoulders of an Arkarian, fire an arrow, and continue to their next target.

I never knew they could move like that. It was amazing to see them operate. I never got the chance to battle one before in this kind of battle, especially as they were on the other side of the courtyard. As for the Dekams, I slew a few; however, I do not think it was a fair battle because I caught them from behind.

The duration will come when I battle the Dekams again. In that span, I will enjoy the battle. When the rest of the clans entered, we all realized we were being overrun. This was when we ran into the main keep.

******

9

THE ENCOUNTER

Blinking his eyes, Draka looks up to see himself once again back in this place. He shakes his head because he said he would never again come here. They step up to the doors, which open by themselves.

The sound of their opening echoes through the halls. The three Adeians slowly enter the main keep. The air still holds the aroma of death. It is like opening a crypt that has over two thousand cycles. The hollow sound of their footsteps added to the voices of souls long gone makes it eerie.

Draka cannot help but stare off into what looks like endless darkness. He looks around as if he is looking for something, or maybe something is looking for him.

The hallway leading toward the throne room is poorly lit and longer than he remembers. Yet the light is enough to see the horror and the transformation of the Kazar.

Many of the passageways are now eternally blocked from the ceiling falling in. The pitch-blackness along the hallway, which seems to have taken over the Kazar, appears to submerge column tops. Draka is very tall for an Adeian. As he walks down the hallway, the blackness over his head seems to reach down to consume him.

He stands nine cycles of the Yohba tree plus ten at his last turn of being. His rough, dark skin has many scars from all the battles he has engaged in. His large, muscular frame supports shoulders that spread five cycles of the Yohb.

The girth of his neck is the envy of most Yohba trees. His sturdy arms are built to wield his heavy sword along with his battle ax with ease, and his legs are strong enough to sustain them all. *{**Arkarians refer to this as the built of a warrior.**}*

All this, along with his solid blue eyes, conveys the curious combination of friendship and death, each quality reserved for specific beings. His steely expression softens, conveying a willingness to extend this friendship to those he regards as true.

His helmet hides his hair, but when removed, it descends past his shoulders. It is like the Turn of the Twins when they are in hiding, it ripples like still water when a cool breeze blows across the top {Dark Purple and wavy}. Bushy mustache with thick sideburns attempts to cover his face from the world.

The armor he wears is like a second skin, covering him from his neck to the soles of his feet. Across the expanse of his back is his most trusted ally, an enormous, ancient, double-sided sword. *{**This is a tale for another duration.**}* He also carries ten daggers, tactically placed all over his body.

His ability as a warrior is well known throughout Clan Adeian. Because of his skills, most know of him, and many fear him. However, of those, most would be delighted to bring him down but are afraid to try.

Walking through the halls, a song runs through his mind of yet another tale of a battle long gone.

'ACROSS THE VAST Q'FAHTI
THEY CAME TO STOP THE BATTLES OF THE CLANS.
EMERGING OUT OF THE TUNNELS THEY RODE,
FOR MATOCA'S HORDES DARED TO STAND.
THE SKY BECAME DARK WITH ARKARIAN ARROWS.
THIS BROUGHT MUCH PAIN AND SO MUCH SORROW.

*ALL CLANS OF ALL THE LANDS GOT TOGETHER TO BATTLE
MATOCA AND HIS BAN.
HEARTS FILLED WITH PASSION; THE CLANS CONTINUED.
THE HORDE FELT THEIR DUNAMIS POWER,
THIS CHANGED THEIR COURSE AND THEIR DIRECTION,
BUT MANY ADEIANS WERE SLAIN BECAUSE OF MATOCA'S
OBSESSION.'*

'An obsession? Not many knew of this obsession. The few who did are now slain. Those who remain are afraid to ask. One of these durations, I will ask. When I feel like it. However, I believe Scarra knows more than she claims.'

He turns slightly to look at Scarra, who walks behind him. With a slight nod, he turns, facing forward again, leaving Scarra to her thoughts.

She looks up, and a cold shiver runs down her spine as she approaches the ingress. Involuntarily, she looks up at the ceiling. To her, it looks as if the Firelight has forever abandoned this place. The darkness seems to be reaching down to claim anyone foolish enough to walk these halls ever again.

With every step, her mind reflects on cycles long gone--that duration of the Battle with the Clans.

'It is as if the power of the Veloian Users is still strong; As if somehow their power has increased in some way.'

What astonished her more were Matoca's new powers. *'How did he get so strong?'* It still bothers her about his powers. *'I have always been stronger than he was, and that aggravated him.'*

Her eyes dart from side to side, and with every step, her memory seems to reveal more of the battle, especially with the Users.

'I remember the utterance of every User who spoke an uttering. Then the destruction of the Kazar came, and we barely escaped with our lives, those of us who made it out.

If it were not for Derla's Sire, I would be nothing but a memory within these walls. How then did Matoca survive?' She continued to walk as a distant memory flashed in her mind.

One memory she would rather forget. This one took place during the duration before the battle. It was the duration that she left Matoca's Kazar, vowing never to return--that last duration that she shared Matoca's bed.

Something was troubling him, but when she asked, he never told her. She had news for him and hoped it would put him in a better mood.

His reaction to the news sent her running out of the room into the great hall, now known as his throne room. She remembers the pain she felt as she sat there on the floor, crying. Many cycles came and went before that battle, now, just like then, she has broken her vow.

The flame she has for him is still strong no matter how hard she tries to stay away, all he has to do is call. *'I cannot believe I am back in this place.'*

She walks past Draka and smiles to herself while at the same duration, she tries to keep Yar at bay. *'I hope this meeting does not turn out unsightly, if it does, will Matoca be strong enough to control it?'*

As the thought enters her mind, her eye flashes brightly in the poorly lit hall, but it dims just as quickly. She hopes none of the others paid any attention.

However, her wishes are in vain, because Draka sees it, and slowly his hand moves away from his dagger when the light dims. As much as he admires Scarra, with what has been going on, he is not in a trusting mood. He studies her and notices she has not changed much.

'Her beauty still radiates; her skin is still smooth. She is much lighter than me. Look how her skin glows beneath her gown of red and brown. Is this why Matoca cannot leave her alone?

She only stands about seven cycles of the Yohba tree, plus ten at her last turn of being. I always liked her brown hair, how it flows down to her waist, rippling impatiently like a strong breeze across still waters.'

Bringing up the rear is Yar, who smiles thinking as he watches Draka's hand move from his dagger, *'That half-breed is still jumpy, maybe this meeting will be fun after all.'*

Yar stands one Yohb shorter than Draka, plus five at his last turn of being. He is naught but a shade darker than Scarra, with hair color and texture as hers. However, his eyes are solid red.

His frame is almost as muscular as Draka's, but medium in size compared to Draka's huge frame. His shoulders spread four cycles of a Yohba tree. Across the top of his mouth is a thin mustache. The attire he wears reflects his demeanor.

Both his pants and vest are dark, with a white silk-like shirt made from Yohba roots. He has two daggers at his side, a gift from his Sire for completing his Dunamis training many thousands of cycles ago.

Speeding up, Yar makes his way past Draka, making sure he brushes up against him to show he does not fear him.

Passing Scarra, he whispers, "You should have uttered your words." Stopping to face them with mischief dancing in his eyes, he continues. "I think I should be in charge of this little group. After all, I am the oldest, the strongest, and the smartest."

Draka glares scornfully at him. With a few quick steps, he overtakes him, in a low voice, he spat the word,

"Fool."

Yar's eyes glow slowly as his anger begins to grow. Turning to Draka he asks, "Who are you calling a fool, half-breed?"

Draka stops in his tracks and turns to Yar with a murderous expression on his face. The look startles Yar. He lowers his eyelids over his glowing eyes.

To calm his nerves, he laughs. "HA! HA! HA! What are you thinking of doing?"

In one smooth motion, Draka pulls his sword, grabs Yar, and throws him up against the wall, before answering, "Do not make the mistake of using your senseless power on me, Yar, or I will send your head rolling down this hall."

Yar tries to squirm out of his grip, but Draka presses his sword tightly against his neck until it draws blood. Intensely, Draka watches as the blood rolls slowly down his sword. He leans into Yar, whispering in his ear, "Pray your first utterance works, for you will not get another chance."

Yar tries to concentrate on his utterance. His eyes glow brighter, casting Draka's shadow against the wall behind him. As Yar's eyes shift to the shadow on the wall, he is then reminded of the Battle with the Veloians. He remembers facing two Veloians and how he was overwhelmed while trying to fend them off.

His mind quickly shifts back to that battle with the Veloians. If it were two Adeians, he could have just waved his hands, and they would have been tossed away like paper. But...

******

10

YAR'S BATTLE

. . . they were not, Yar found himself standing in front of these two Veloians. They were not his age. They looked at least five hundred cycles younger than he was. They stood there watching him, daring him to make a move.

The one to his left held out his hand, and a plasmatic glow started to form, then burst into flames. While the other to his right pulled on the static in the air to form a lightning bolt. Then both of them raised their hands and aimed in Yar's direction.

Knowing he could not take on one Veloian by himself, nevertheless two, Yar did the only thing he could think of, he ran for cover. The Veloians released their energy.

The combination created a powerful blast that sent all three of them flying backward, in opposite directions. Yar could not believe how fast they were back on their feet.

'I do not want to fight them. They are too strong. They battle with such fury as if their powers are moving with their actions.'

Reaching down to his side, Yar pulled his sword. Quickly, he rushed the one to his left and swung his sword with what he thought to be true. However, the Veloian proved to be faster, shifting out of sight {meaning moves to another dimension}. Yar stopped, astonished at what he had just seen.

Without thinking, the Veloian User had shifted. Yar stood there, sword in hand, just staring into the area where the Veloian had been standing. He had to concentrate before he could even move. He forgot about the other Veloian User who at this duration was about to fire another energy bolt.

The glowing of the Veloian's hand alerted him to spin around when the Veloian released the bolt. Yar jumped out of the way of the bolt as it shot past. The intensity of the bolt temporarily blinded him.

The other Veloian stepped out of the shift after the bolt passed and struck Yar in the chest, sending him hurtling to the ground. Grabbing his chest, he tried to stand, but because of his lack of physical strength. He fell back to the ground. Yar rubbed his eyes and then tried to open them. He got a glimpse of the two Veloian Users closing in on him.

Both of them prepared to fire another bolt at him. Fear overcame him as he saw this duration to be his last. From where he fell in connection to the ground, he raised his hand to block the onslaught, when deep inside he felt a force as if a door opened to the next level of his Dunamis Powers.

A brilliant light surrounded his body as the Powers of the Dunamis began to grow within him. When his eyes cleared, the only thing he saw were shadows of the two Veloians facing him, who would never again see the Firelight.

On that Turn of the Twins, his power grew tenfold.

******

11

BLOOD DRAWN

"Let him go!" Yar snaps out of his trance when he hears Scarra's voice commanding Draka. Yar blinks his eyes to see Draka still holding the sword at his throat.

Scarra continues, "You know Matoca will not like it if you slay him now, especially since he has not seen him in many cycles." She pauses before adding, "And in his Kazar."

She takes a moment to look around when she finishes her statement, as if to find Matoca behind her. Yar's blood begins to flow a little more freely as Draka's sword bites in a little deeper.

Squinting, Draka glances toward Scarra. Aggressively, he pushes Yar harder against the wall making him gasp for air, then reluctantly, he lets go, dropping him to the floor.

"Yes, we must not mess up Matoca's Kazar with the blood of a Rookile..." Draka replies scornfully.

Then he turns his attention back to Yar and continues in agreement, "To add more blood would be a shame. Let us not forget what this Kazar cost us all." He looks back at Scarra.

"Must I remind you of your Sire's slaying by the Hunters?" As the words escape his mouth, it brings back to Scarra the memories of the events which took place all those cycles long ago. The color on her face fades as she remembers the chaos on that Turn of the Twins...

******

******

12

REMEMBERING

The doors to the great hall burst open, and a young lord named Sham came running in, yelling at Matoca and the others. Inside the hall were many Adeians, with those few Matoca had appointed, lords.

Some of the lords' names were Ba'Dal, Scarra, Cy'Raa, and Reela, along with a few others. They all turned to look at Sham as he stopped.

Gasping for air, he took a deep breath before speaking again. "Lord Matoca, the Veloian Hunters are overpowering the Wards. The Dekams are right behind them, the Arkarians have already taken the towers along with the battlements."

Matoca looked toward the open doors, and with a wave of his hand, they closed. He put a protective shield around them.

Turning to Sham, he asked urgently, "What of their Users? Where are the Users?" Sham glanced toward Ba'Dal, his flame. She studied his face, and without saying a word, she knew they could not win this battle. Sham turned to Matoca and then answered.

"My Lord, I did not see the Veloian Users. The Dekams were directly behind the Hunters. My Wards gave their lives so I may bring this information to you."

Nodding, Matoca turned to the others and spoke. "We need to split up to divide the Clans. This way we can take them out in one group at a duration. Once we have taken care of the Veloian Hunters and the Dekams, we look for their Users. Last will be the Arkarians. They will all fall into my hands."

Some of the Adeians in the hall cheered when Matoca spoke. However, a few thought what he said to be madness, so they spoke out against him.

One of these voices is Reela, who said. "My lord, we cannot win this battle. We must flee, regroup, and come up with another plan."

Reela turned to those who were with him, as another stepped forward to speak. His name was Cy'Raa, Scarra's Sire.

He said, "This is true; we will not be able to take on all the Clans at once. Some of us must stay and battle. This will give some duration for the rest of us to escape."

Matoca, hearing this, did not like the idea of them undermining him. He had never trusted Reela, but he did not think that Cy'Raa would act against him as well. Knowing very well that Cy'Raa and Reela's voices could influence the others, he could not do anything against them, at least for now.

He knew now was not the duration to speak out on this, especially if he was to have the others with him. He looked at Cy'Raa and Reela and thought.

'I must go along with what they said. But when the duration is right, I will deal with them.'

A false smile spread on his face as he looked at the others in agreement, then he said, "You are right."

All of the murmurings stopped when those words left his mouth. Many stood there in astonishment. The disbelief on their faces said it all. Matoca took advantage of this. With a strange smile, he said, "Both of you are right." Thinking quickly, he devised another plan using their ideas, but with a little twist.

Instead, he continued with his plan. "I still think we should split up. This way, the Hunters cannot go after all of us. The groups should be small. Cy'Raa and Reela, I would like both of you to accompany me to my group. I could use both of you to help me come up with any other plans. As for the rest of you..."

Before Matoca could finish speaking, the Veloian Hunters reached the door. Quickly, he spoke an utterance, and another wall of force went up around the doors. All the Adeians in the room said their goodbyes. Then they separated into their groups and headed towards other doors.

At this duration, the Veloian Users broke Matoca's utterance. The doors flew open, and then the Dunamis Powers went flying. The Adeian Wards were the first to enter the battle with the Veloians. As Veloian Users uttered, the Adeian Wards fired arrows.

The destruction of the first waves of arrows was quick. Some of the Veloian Users fell while others struck back. Many of the Adeian Wards fell. In the second wave of Adeian arrows, some more of the Veloian Users lost their lives.

The second wave of Veloian Users released all their utterances, which sent a shock wave throughout the Kazar. Fireballs and lightning bolts were released, but some of the Adeian Users were able to divert what was released. However, most could not.

Without warning, chunks of cement began swirling around the room. Blocks of concrete came crashing down from the walls, the ceiling, and debris from the floor. The rocks crushed and knocked both Adeian wards and Users alike, slaying them instantly.

Some of the wards were able to move out of the way. Others screamed in agony as the elements hit. Adeian Wards with the Users returned fire. Again, the arrows flew in the direction of the Veloian Users. During this duration, Veloian Hunters sprinted away from their User's sides and then fired their arrows.

The Hunters' arrows flew up in the air and entered directly in the path of the Adeian arrows, hitting them, snapping them in two. Some of them sent in other directions away from Veloian Users. Many of the Veloian arrows struck true, hitting the heads of the Adeian archers.

At this duration, the Dekams ran in heading toward what was left of the Adeian Wards. Before the Wards could draw their swords, the Dekams were upon them. The battle did not last long because the Dekams cut down the Adeians with ease, and the few survivors fled.

Matoca, along with the Users with him, came into the battle by sending their utterance in the direction of the Dekams. Many of the Dekams were slain along with some of the Adeian Wards.

Seeing this, the Veloian Users used this opportunity to release another round of utterances. This duration went in the direction of Matoca and those standing with him.

Matoca saw the onslaught and shifted slightly out of the way. As for those who were not able to move fast enough, they were engulfed in many forms of Dunamis utterances. The Hunters moved to the side, firing their arrows toward Matoca and the rest.

As Scarra saw this, she was able to divert some of the arrows, however, many hit their mark, and a few more Adeians fell to the ground. Matoca pulled his sword to fight off some of the Dekams who survived his Users' utterances. He yelled at Scarra when he saw what she did.

"Scarra, take your group and get out of here." He blocked the swing of a sword to his right.

She yelled, "No, I will not leave without my Sire."

She released a blast of fire towards a few Dekams that were heading towards her, while Matoca blocked another sword to his left.

He yelled back. "I will make sure he gets out of here. Now go."

Cy'Raa turning to her shouted, "Do not worry, we will get out, now go. My flame goes with you."

She watched as Matoca blocked a sword heading towards her Sire. Derla's Sire pulled her into a room away from the fighting. The last thing she saw was the roof caving in, and then they all ran out the hidden door in the wall.

******

13

THRONEROOM

Coming out of her memories, a tear escapes her eye. She looks at Draka and notices the sadness in his eyes. Then she remembers that he lost Tri'Ela, on that turn, as well. Although he seems hardened against everything, his loss is just as great as hers.

Wiping away the tears from her eyes, she says, "I do not think there is any need to continue."

With a weak smile, she gently places her hand on Draka's sword. He turns to her to see another tear rolling down her cheek. Releasing Yar, he sheathes his sword and walks away. As he wipes the blood from his neck, Yar heals himself, while he mutters, "You are lucky she stopped you, for I was about to..."

Yar never got the chance to finish his sentence. Draka's sword parts the air, only to stop at his neck, ready to relieve his body of the burden of his head.

Startled, Scarra yells out, "DRAKA, NO."

Yar knows he has only one chance, so he concentrates on his utterance. But he is no fool. Seeing how close Draka is to him. He knows that at this close range, his power would be useless, for he realizes that he, too, would be slain by his powers. As much as he would like to see Draka slain by his hands, he would wait for the right duration.

The Kazar walls start to shake as a thunderous voice echoes throughout, saying.

"STOP!"

Yar watches as the sword moves and then vanishes into the dark. He hears Draka sheathing it and walking away.

Again, the voice sounds. **"ALL WILL STOP NOW!"**

This duration, the thunderous voice did not shake the walls. It is coming from the throne room. Scarra walks past Draka heading off in that direction.

Yar shakes off what almost happened to him. *'The half-breed got faster,'* he thinks, as he follows behind the other two.

Approaching the throne room, the doors open by themselves. The light emerging from the room is so bright that they shield their eyes until they adjust. Upon entering, Draka notices that the room is not lit by torches, but by an ominous glow from above. Near the back of the room is a table with three chairs, one on each side with a throne at the head.

Walking to the table, he can see the throne a little better. It is on a raised dais, made of gold with emeralds, diamonds, rubies, and pearls embedded in the arms and the back. The head of a Lentar adorns the top.

Sitting on the throne is Matoca, his broad shoulders almost touching the sides. He is wearing a hood, which masks his facial features, revealing only glowing, red eyes, which accentuate them and make them more menacing in the shadows.

"Come sit down," he says. During this duration, his voice is back to its normal, deceptive tone.

Even though he is sitting, Draka remembers the way he looked, about average height, his appearance was nothing more than that of an average Adeian.

His skin is smooth and dark. *'I remember his aura, how it conveyed power that demanded respect and obedience from all he encountered. I wonder if he still has it?'* Draka asks himself.

The three of them make their way to the seats he indicates. Draka takes a quick scan around the room. The glow above makes it difficult to see if there is anything at the edges of the oval room. Even with the destruction, one can see that Matoca was busy rebuilding it with his Dunamis.

The tiles on the floor still show the image of the compass. The original names for the poles still stand out strong; Zuroth [north], Bimu' [east], Miu [west], and Uroth [south] all written in the ancient language.

In the darkness beyond the light, Draka notices the pillars with draperies that still adorn the walls above.

'He rearranged the room so that his throne would be positioned towards the Zuroth, the exits would be at each pole.' He is thinking this while taking notes on the exit doors, realizing from the light spilling out beneath them that they are all closed.

'If I remember correctly, there is another secret door on the wall just behind his seat. It should be covered with a tapestry.'

He takes special notice of the spaces between the pillars lining the walls of this hall.

'There is some faint movement coming from those statues. Ah, they are Wards. Even with the great number of them outside, he still feels he needs more protection.

What could he be so afraid of? Why have so many Wards? I do believe Matoca is afraid of something. Could it be the Veloians? Maybe that is why he feels he needs to be protected here as well.'

Although he cannot see any Wards clearly, he is guessing they are adorned much like those outside, with black armor and hoods. The normal weapons they carry will be two double-edged swords with two daggers to match.

As they take their seats, Draka notices that he is sitting opposite Yar, while Scarra sits opposite Matoca. He looks at her noticing her flush, painted lips are red as the sky before twilight.

He likes how it brings out the golden hue of her eyes. The cape she wears enhances her shapely body, revealing the slimness of her arms and legs. Her cape itself is a status symbol of an Adeian Adept, fashioned to match the color of her eyes.

{**An Adept is an Adeian who is skilled in their craft, within the User Class.**}

Her Sire made her this cape as a present for commencing her passage to Adept. Only an Adeian Adept can create this kind of cape, made by draining some of their Adept life force and bonding it with the material's natural essence.

The Adept then utters a protection over the cape. When worn, the utterance is empowered. Because of the merging of the owner's life force with the natural essence, both the cape and the owner make the cape invulnerable to certain Dunamis Powers, all projectiles, also some swords.

Were he still alive, her Sire's eyes would fill with tears to see how powerful she had become. Draka shifts his attention toward the throne, looking into Matoca's eyes, he asks, "Matoca, we thought you to be slain in the last battle with the Veloian Users. What happened to you?"

"Why should you be concerned with what happened to me, or what I am doing? Do you wish me slain?" Matoca asks coolly.

Draka shakes his head, responding, "No, it is just that after the battle with the Users, you seemed to have vanished. We are... I am curious to know what happened to you. Besides, I did not ask what you are doing."

Slowly, Matoca's eyes glow a little brighter as he answers. "I did not vanish. I just wanted to take myself out of the way for a while to regroup. If that is OKAY WITH YOU."

The table vibrates; dust fills the air; the light above slightly dims. Matoca inhales deeply. Everything slowly goes back to normal, and his eyes stop glowing.

"You are all here on this Turn of the Twins because I bid you here."

Still leaning on the table, Draka clenched his fist and looked squarely at Matoca while saying in a stern voice. "What do you mean by saying YOU bid us? You have been gone too long. Many things have happened. You no longer have the right to bid on any of us."

Leering at him, Yar leans in with that scornful grin, he says to Draka, "What he means half-breed..."

Draka's head snaps towards Yar. Eyes blazing, he snarls at him. In a dangerous tone, he snaps, "He can speak for himself. He does not need the words of a Sana."

Yar looks at Draka. He watches expectantly as his hand moves to his side. Turning to Matoca, Yar's eyes flash when he looks at him.

Then he closes them before turning his full attention back towards Draka. Pretending that Draka had not spoken, he says, "As I was saying, if Matoca wishes us here, then here we should be. It is not your place to question him."

Still looking at Draka, whose hand remains at his side, he finishes. "It does not matter how long he has been gone."

Turning back to Matoca, Yar continues. "If it were not for Matoca, the Arkarians, or worse, the Dekams would have made us into bond-servants. Or we could have gotten lucky, like Tri'Ela, slain by the Veloians." Yar looks at Scarra with a silly grin, saying, "Right?"

Scarra jumps back as Draka slams his fist on the table, bares his teeth, he addresses Yar. "Why has my flame's name crossed your lips, you infested bile of a Gargon! {**A creature that lives in the wetlands**}. You have no right, nor permission, to utter my flame's name!" With a low voice shaking in anger, he challenges Yar.

Nearly overturning his chair in his effort to stand, Yar yells. "How dare you? How would you like to meet your flame again, and feast with the Dark One much sooner than you plan to?"

Yar raises his right hand, which bursts into flames as he continues. "I will say any name I wish to at any duration, you cannot stop me."

Still baring his teeth, Draka slowly pulls a dagger, holding it in an Adeian grip {**Blade pointed back against his forearm**}. With quick reflexes, he places his hand on the table, his body following.

His eyes fixed on Yar's burning hand, he says in a low, challenging voice. "Do it! And we will dine with the Dark One together." Slowly, Yar pulls his hand back, preparing to release the fireball.

Draka raises his dagger. Every muscle in his body tightens as he crouches, ready to pounce. Suddenly, two Wards press their swords mercilessly against Yar's neck, forcing him to diminish his uttering.

Draka stops in mid-action, forced to put the dagger away. Both of their bodies slam back into their seats by a force so strong their chairs creak in distress. They both look in Matoca's direction to see him sitting there, slowly closing his hands.

"You should all remember," he says, looking at all of them scornfully. "I put you all where you are now," pointing directly at Draka, "And I can easily take it away."

Scarra looks at both of them fighting to hold back the tears, while Matoca continues. "Now let us begin this discussion without anyone leaving their seats again."

He waves his hands. Immediately, a ball of emerald, green light appears on the table that unfolds into a small map revealing all the realms within Icka's Domain.

The source less light above them dims as Matoca continues. "The reason I summon you here is to show you my entire plan. I have been watching the fighting amongst yourselves for what little land you have. This must stop.

(The battles Matoca is referring to are mainly between Yar and Draka.) Let us redirect our aggression to come together to conquer all of this." He waves his hands over the whole map on the table, saying. "It can all be in our control."

Draka sits back in his seat. Turning his head slightly towards Matoca, he says,

"This is a good idea. But how are you going to get all of Clan Adeian to unite? Our lands hold less than half a million warriors. Now, if you can get an audience with Sham. Maybe you can get him to agree to help.

He has a large number of warriors because of the land he controls. Then I could see your plan working, because unlike some of us who believe your every word..."

Draka lets it soak in as he glances in Yar's direction. Continuing, he says,

"There are those who did not forget the last duration you tried something like this. It made the Clans come together, led by the Hunters, to stop you. How can you be sure the Veloians will not do it again?"

He pauses for a moment to take a breath before adding.

"OK, let us say this plan does work. What will be in it for us? Who will be in charge?"

Smiling broadly, Matoca says, "Why, I would of course!"

Scarra looks at Matoca sharply. In a challenging tone, she asks. "Why you? Why not one of us? She points to herself, then motions to Yar, then Draka. Realizing how hard she sounds when she speaks, she tones down her voice. "I mean, you do not have to do all the work."

Smiling, Matoca responds. "Because, my dear, this is my plan. I have the power to destroy all of you if I wish. However, I would rather have us work together. Besides, it would be a shame to see your head separated from your lovely body. I rather like it the way it is." His eyes flash disagreeably in the hood.

Feeling left out, Yar thinks he has to say something, however inane. He asks in a sarcastic tone, with a grin that matches. "OK, if you are going to be in charge? What I would like to know is, who will be second? In case you vanish again?"

Pointing to Scarra, Matoca answers easily. "Why, Scarra of course." Then he points toward Draka, then Yar, and continues, "As for who will be after her, I will leave it up to both of you to decide. I am sure you can do that all by yourself. But do not take too long."

"What would you consider being too long?" Yar asks again, in the same sarcastic tone.

Draka shakes his head thoughtfully. *'This does not feel like a good idea. However, I will play along for now. It could get interesting. Maybe I might get the chance to slay one of them.'* He looks at Yar, then at Matoca, who continues. "You will know."

Looking in Yar's direction, Matoca scowls.

Leaning to his left, Draka says, "Now, all this is good, but we still have a problem. Like the Veloian Hunters who still dwell within the Q-Farhti' Forest, do not forget about their Users, or did you? I hope not, because they are the ones who redesigned your Kazar."

Draka raises his hands above his head, indicating the room around them. Then he continues, "Do you remember the first duration I went into the Q-Farhti' Forest..." His voice trailed off as he remembered...

Scarra and Yar turned towards Draka, listening with interest. Some of what Draka is about to say, they already knew. The rest will take them by surprise, especially Scarra. It all happened during the first duration of Matoca's utterance.

In the first battle, Draka was in charge of, no one knew Matoca ordered his actions, not even the Veloians, at least, not then. As he talks, memories of that duration flood back.

******

14

FIRST ENCOUNTER

Draka rode into the Kazar gates and dismounted. To his right, he noticed a Ban of Wards getting ready for battle. He walked into the Kazar and headed directly for the throne room. When he entered, he saw Matoca in a meeting, talking to Sham with a few others.

He stopped and waited for them to finish because he was not a part of their group at that duration. As far as he was concerned, he was still a bondservant to them. He had no idea what was about to happen to him, that his status in Matoca's group was about to change.

When the meeting ended, the group broke up. That was when he looked at Scarra. She was smiling at him in a way that made him a little uneasy. Then Matoca called him over to the center of the group.

If he had known then what he knows now, he probably would not have taken the position he was about to be offered, but at that duration, he wanted to be a part of the group so badly he would have done anything. When Matoca smiled, he realized that it was the first duration he had ever seen him smile. It was not a pleasant sight.

Yar stood on Scarra's left. The look on his face was one that he would not have liked to see if he were alone with him. Draka knew that whatever it was that Matoca was going to say to him, Yar would not like it. That alone was worth a lot to him.

Draka walked up to Matoca and gave him full honors. [This is done to someone in a higher rank, by making fists with both hands crossed over the heart, then slamming the fists against the chest before kneeing.]

Matoca placed his hand on Draka's head and then said,

"On this Turn of the Firelight in front of all these witnesses, I declare that Draka of Adeian is hereby known as Lord Draka. He is to receive all the privileges that go along with this rank. As of now and forevermore until I dismiss you, or you are slain, you shall hold this position. Now stand, Lord Draka."

All the other Adeian lords came over to congratulate him, all that was, except Yar. He went the other way, but Draka saw his face before he walked away. He could not help smiling. He was no longer a bond-servant.

He also knew this made Yar disgusted to the pit of his being. They are now equal. After everyone gave their congratulations, Matoca walked up to him again and led him out towards the courtyard.

Once outside, Matoca said, "I am glad to have given you the status of 'Lord.' This way I can give you a very important charge…"

"I will do what you command."

A sly smile creased Matoca's face. They walked towards a Ban of Wards standing by their Zaruses, ready to mount. Stopping, Matoca turned to him and then said, "Your charge is to take this Ban, go into the Q-Farhti' Forest, and defeat the Veloians."

Draka stopped and turned to him, a look of surprise on his face… He asked, "I thought we did not know where the Veloians were. If they have to slay each other, why do we have to interfere? When you said 'defeat,' do you mean the entire clan?"

Matoca tilted his head slightly to the left, curiously regarding Draka with an underhanded look, answering, "Yes."

Draka stared suspiciously at Matoca.

Matoca nodded his head and continued, "You are going to make sure that they do not come to the aid of the Dekams or the Arkarians when we battle them. We are not strong enough to battle all three clans at the same duration. The Dekams and the Arkarians are not battling each other like the Veloians.

"If we strike the Arkarians first, we can wipe them out. Then we will not have to battle them when the Dekams come. The truth is, the Veloians are the ones who caused this utterance. They have to be defeated for this to stop. If we do not stop them now, we will never be able to do it again."

Matoca paused for a moment knowing how much Draka wanted to be a part of the group. Matoca was hoping he would jump at the chance to do anything.

Once more, Draka took the opportunity to ask, "Why not get the help of the Dekams and the Arkarians?"

Looking at him, Matoca realized that he was no fool. *I have to be careful about this one. I can see that he is not easily moved!* Shaking his head, Matoca replied,

"Because my young one, the Dekams, along with the Arkarians, are under the same utterance as we are. The Veloians started this; if we do not stop them, we will all be slain. I know how much you fancy Tri'Ela. I give my word that I will do everything in my power to keep her safe."

Matoca said this in the hope that Draka would not think anything negative of him, at least not yet. He continued, "That is until you come back from the Q-Farhti' Forest. I need you to do this for our clan to survive and for Tri'Ela. I am counting on you."

Draka looked at Matoca and nodded reluctantly in agreement. More than anything, he wanted Tri'Ela safe.

He turned and walked to the Ward holding his Zarus, Torian. Before he mounted, he stopped, turned back to Matoca one more duration, asking, "Why me? Why not Sham, Hykrr, La'Lek, or Ma'Dro, or one of the others?

They are more capable than I am. Besides, I just became a lord, and they have been lords for many cycles now. I do not have as many skills as the rest."

Again, Matoca shook his head, saying, "I have been watching you for quite some while now. I believe you can carry out this charge. That is why I wanted you to become a lord. Now go, show me that I did not make an oversight. I will await your return."

Matoca turned and walked away, leaving Draka to think about what he had just said. Turning back to the Ward, Draka took the reins and mounted his Zarus reluctantly. He turned to take one last look at Matoca's hurriedly retreating form, walking away, never looking back. Draka rode off, followed by his Ban of fifty thousand.

As he rode, he thoughtfully tried to understand the nature of his mission, if whatever Matoca told him about the Veloians was true.

'Since the Veloians were battling each other. It would be easier for me and my Ban to battle them without many casualties; hopefully, we can catch them off guard.'

It took his Ban several turns to reach the edge of the forest, only stopping to feed the Zaruses. Upon arriving, Draka called for them to dismount. They marched warily into the Q-Farhti' Forest. Leaving their Zaruses at the edge of the forest made it easier for them to travel into the trees silently.

Slowly, they approached the Veloian encampment. They could hear the sound of battle coming from the area. Stopping a good distance from the encampment, Draka sent Entes, his second, whom Matoca appointed with a scouting party to see what they might be going into.

The party came back to report to Draka. Entes said,

"My lord, they are battling each other with such ferocity. They do not even know we are here. We can very easily enter the camp and slay them without losing many of our Wards. Matoca was right. If we are to strike now, there would not be much of a resistance."

Draka looked at the Adeian bending down next to him. *'I have seen this one before, though not as much as the others. My question is, why is he here? Better yet, why did Matoca send him? I need to keep him in front of me until we get back.'*

Draka nodded his head in satisfaction with this plan. Then he said to Entes.

"What do you think is the best way to battle them, without losing much of our Ban?"

Entes cleared an area on the ground. He mapped out the Veloians' camp and then said.

"If we split our Ban into four, we can hit them on all sides at the same duration while they are still battling each other. We can have the conquest before they can react."

Nodding his head in agreement with this plan, Draka added, "I want you to take half and go on the other side." *'This way I can keep my eye on you,'* he thought, as he continued speaking.

"When you are in place give me a signal, then we start our battle. Nodding in agreement, Entes got up, and along with Draka, they moved toward the rest of the Ban.

After they split the Ban into two groups, Entes took his Ban to the other side of the Veloians' camp. Once in position, he gave Draka the signal. Then the battle with the Veloians began. Draka stood in the back of his group, not paying them any attention, but watching Entes.

His Ban moved through the camp with little opposition, slaying all Veloians within blades' reach. Draka started to step out toward an opening leading to the camp clearing. When a great force pushed him backward with such a force, it made him fall to the ground.

Quickly, he regained his footing to the sound of screaming. He looked to his left and then to his right, only to see his Ban running away from the camp. Moving the bushes out of his way, he was astonished at what he saw in the camp and those who were still standing—only the Veloians.

Many of his Ban were lying on the ground and did not get the chance to stand before an arrow found its mark. Wave after wave, Veloian Dunamis crashed into one member of his Ban after another.

He watched some of his Ban battle the Veloian Hunters, while their Users' utterances hit them both, their Hunters along with members of his Ban. Only their Hunters walked away.

That was when Draka realized that Veloian Dunamis did not work on their Hunters. He continued to watch as both the Veloian Users and Hunters turned their aggression on the rest of his Ban as they ran off into the forest.

He waited until the last of the Veloians ran off in pursuit before moving. As he moved through the forest, he shook his head at what he saw.

'I do not believe what I am seeing. Their Dunamis did not affect their Hunters. Why? I have seen what Adeian Users do to other Adeians. They did not survive. So, how is it that the Veloian Users' utterances did not harm their Hunters?

I never did like the Dunamis. Maybe that is the reason I cannot stand Yar. No!' he shook his head. *I just do not like Yar, period. Besides, that does not explain how the Veloian Hunters were able to walk away from their Users' Dunamis.'*

He stopped for a moment, looking around, his blade at the ready. Cautiously, he scanned the surrounding forest looking for movement of any kind. Something did not seem right. The hair on the back of his neck began to stand on end. Crouching low, sword in his left hand, he reached for a dagger with his right.

Cautiously, he looked around the forest. His eyes shifted from tree to tree until an arrow flew towards him. He blocked it with the sword, but the second one hit him in the left shoulder, sending him spinning.

His right hand pulled the dagger. He threw it in the direction of the arrows before he hit the ground. The dagger hit another arrow headed toward him, splitting it in two, and then continued its journey toward the owner, shattering his bow.

The Veloian Hunter dropped the bow, pulled his saber, and jumped from tree to tree towards Draka. Getting up, Draka blocked the first strike of the Hunter. However, the second one struck him in the back.

The force sent him forward. He could feel the warmth of his blood soaking his clothes.

Stopping, he turned to face his attacker, who was already swinging again. The only thing he could do was block one strike after another. Each block sent him one step backward until he backed up into a tree. On the next swing, Draka ducked, moving out of the way. This allowed Hunter's saber to become stuck in the tree.

Draka took this duration to swing his sword, hitting the saber and breaking it. His second swing went to the mid-section of the Hunter, who jumped back, causing Draka to miss.

The Hunter pulled his dagger as he jumped on Draka. The impact sent them both to the ground. He struck. Draka held his sword with both hands, blocking the dagger. Then he hit the Hunter with the hilt of his sword.

Rolling off, the Hunter stood, turned, and dove back toward Draka, who held his sword in front of him, unable to move quickly out of the way. The Hunter fell on the sword, slaying himself. The body of the Hunter, along with Draka, fell to the ground.

He lay there trying to catch his breath. *I cannot believe the speed of the Hunter. If they are all that fast, we do not have any chance of defeating them,'* he thought, regaining his self-control. He pulled his sword out of the slain Hunter.

Standing on semi-shaky legs, he began to work his way cautiously through the forest. He had never been much when it came to asking the High-One for anything. However, he is hoping the High-One would keep the Veloians at bay until he gets out of the forest.

Draka was disoriented, tired, hurt, bleeding, and anxious that he might run into another Veloian like the first. He lost his sense of direction, realizing that instead of heading out, he could be going deeper into the forest.

He stopped for a moment to regain his bearings because it was getting dark. His eyes darted right, left, then all around searching for Veloians, who could be anywhere, even in the forest canopy.

Seeing lights between the tree trunks, Draka used this as a guide. He trudged wearily until he emerged from the edge of the forest as the Turn of the Twins began to reveal themselves.

He looked toward the Jatego and saw campfires at the base. As fast as he could, he headed in that direction.

'I hope I am not heading to the wrong campfire,' he thought as he arrived at the camp. He entered the area cautiously and looked around. He was happy to see that most of his Ban was still around.

Coming closer, he saw that the campfires spread as far as he could see in all directions.

He made his way to the nearest fire and asked one of the Wards, "How long have you been here?

The Ward replied, "Many of us have been here for a span, others for half. You are the first we have seen since the twins came up."

Draka scanned the area and asked.

"Have you seen Entes?"

A second Ward stood up and then replied.

"My Lord Entes went to report to Lord Matoca. He left just before the twins. I guess he was waiting for you. The last thing he said was for us to wait here until the first Firelight, then gather who survived and head back to the Kazar."

The Ward walked away, leaving Draka with another sitting down by the fire. A third one tended to Draka's wounds while a fourth handed him something to eat. With his wound dressed and some food in his stomach, Draka took a good look at the campfires.

He shook his head, then lay down, staring up at the stars. He wondered what had gone wrong. After a span, he closed his eyes and fell into a sound sleep.

On the next Firelight, Draka woke up to see the Wards heading out. He walked towards them. When he got alongside, he took count of his Ban. For the first duration, he realized he had lost over half of them. Upon returning to Matoca's Kazar, he told him what he learned about the Veloians.

******

15

THE MEETING

Now, Draka looks at Matoca the way he did all those many cycles ago. A thought comes to him. *'I wonder if he remembers what I told him about the Veloians. If he does, what are his plans for them?'*

Scarra looks at Matoca, thinking, *'He must have known that Draka might not return from that battle.'* As she continues watching him, she listens very closely to Draka's story.

'I must know how the Veloian Users were able to use their Dunamis Power against their Hunters without harming them. This is something I must look into when this is all over.'

Yar glances with wonder from Matoca back at Draka, who takes a breath before adding his last question.

"So, with the battles between the clans over, how are you going to deal with a clan that can utter their Dunamis during a battle without harming any of their own? Not to mention, that you must have forgotten their ability to remain **unseen**?"

With a slight grin barely perceptible under his hood, Matoca replies.

"My Dark Ryders will take care of them; of this, I am sure."

Draka shakes his head in disbelief, exploding. "Okay!" Pausing, he continues. "Good, I hope they will be more successful than I was. Now, what about the Dekams living in the Jatego?"

"They are being taken care of as we speak." As he replies, Matoca's voice betrays a sense of annoyance at Draka.

Draka continues to push the issue with yet one more question. "Now, what about the Arkarians living in the lowlands? Their numbers are great because of their outlying Clans--Eekra, U-Inga, Duwala, and Duwumna.

They will not be so easy to defeat, especially if you were to engage any of their clans in battle. The others will come to their aid, and together they can slay us all. Or maybe you have forgotten what happened to the Ban that was sent after U-Inga?"

Matoca eases back in his chair. His eyes shift towards Yar, then to Scarra, before answering, "That was an unfortunate battle."

The icy tone of Matoca's voice sent a numbing feeling through Draka's body.

Yar watches with keen interest, thinking. *Why is the half-breed pushing so hard? It is as if he wants Matoca to use his Dunamis, but why?* He studies Draka intently, and then he notices something.

Hum, there it is. He wants Matoca to use his Dunamis so he can throw his dagger. I hope he does. I would like to see how strong Matoca is if he can stop the dagger. Well, losing the half-breed will not be much of a loss.

Then it came, Draka replies to Matoca furiously.

"Unfortunate! They never had a chance!" Draka's hand moves to the hilt of his sword...

Matoca's eyes dart to Draka's waist and then to his eyes. Sternly, he commands.

"Watch your tone! And yes, it was unfortunate for that Ban. Also unfortunate for the U-Inga Clan, as you recall, their numbers were greatly reduced." Sitting forward in the chair, Matoca repeats with eyes downcast, pretending sorrow, adjusting his voice to suit. "It was unfortunate," Matoca remembers how cunning Draka was, he also remembers how fast as well. He cannot change Draka's wrath, at least not now.

Draka lowers his eyebrows slightly. Moving his hand from his sword, he says through clenched teeth.

"Yes, but their clan remains, even if none of that Ban returned." Continuing in a sterner tone, "There is the rest of our clan. How are you going to get Sham, who made himself the Liege of Zannella, to join you? You must have a better plan if we are to get their help."

Saying this, Draka sits back in his seat. He takes a deep breath, shaking his head, then mutters, loudly enough for Matoca to hear, "Foolish!"

Yar continues to stare at Draka as if he has lost his mind. His eyes shimmer red as he says to Matoca.

"Why not just leave the half-breed out of this? It seems he is not the warrior he claims to be."

Draka sits up in his chair and growls. "I told you not to call me half-breed!" Drawing a dagger, he throws it up into the air. He watches as Yar's eyes follow the dagger.

Quickly, Draka draws another dagger. With a flick of his wrist, the second dagger heads toward Yar in deadly flight.

The dagger flies straight towards Yar's eye. Seeing the dagger within a split duration, Yar can stop it one Ti'fin [inch] away from his eye. It slams into the table as a ball of frost emerges from Yar's mouth, heading straight for Draka. Moving swiftly, he can escape the icy blast.

Without warning, there is a piercing scream of agony. Glancing toward the sound, Draka observes one of the Wards against the wall--frozen. He turns his attention back to Yar and pulls out another dagger. The first one he threw in the air fell, embedding itself into the table.

Yar inhales deeply. Again, he is ready to discharge another ball of frost when a thundering voice echoes throughout the Kazar, rocking everything in the room.

Both Yar and Draka stop what they are doing and then look at Matoca.

"ENOUGH OF THIS!" Matoca demands, eyes glowing bright red as he continues. "Now sit down and let us finish discussing the matter at hand."

Matoca's voice is much lower when he refers to his plan, but the fury in his eyes remains. They retake their seats, allowing Matoca to continue.

"Now, as I was saying. I have a plan that will not fail unless one of you alters it." He looks hard at Yar and Draka in turn, but his stare lingers on Yar. "The first thing I want you all to do is to send me all your warriors."

Yar, seeing how Matoca allows Draka to speak his mind, and the only thing he does is yell. Well, that does not make him feel good at all about the exchange between Matoca and Draka. It makes him very uneasy.

'How could someone such as him confront Matoca without getting something done to him? This is not fair. What does the half-breed have that I do not? He must have something on Matoca.' He thinks.

Unable to contain himself any longer, he shouts.

"What do you mean by sending you all of our warriors? Why should I send you all of my warriors? Why can I not send you half, or better yet, why not just a few? If we did otherwise, who would protect me and...."

With a glance from Matoca, Yar's body crashes up against the wall, destroying the chair beneath him. He falls to the ground, grabbing his chest and gasping for air.

He tries to stand, but the unsteadiness of his legs makes him fall back against the wall. He looks up at Matoca in awe while trying to catch his breath. He barely whispers the words.

"Forgive me." Then he glances in Draka's direction to see if he is smiling at what just happened. But the only thing he sees is Draka leering in Matoca's direction. For the first duration, Yar sees a different, strangely indescribable side of Draka.

'What is this all about? If it was Draka who was slammed against the wall, his chair smashed underneath him, it would have been hilarious, yet he looks at Matoca instead. Why? Does he have something on Matoca? If so, what could it be? I must find out.'

Matoca continues to speak. This duration is undisturbed.

"You will send me all of your warriors. In turn, I will train them to become Dark Ryders. When the training is done, I will send them back to you. All of this will take place in four turns of the Firelight, agreed?"

Unwilling to challenge him any further, they all nod, knowing that while his last words hold the configuration of a question, all three Adeians know it is more of a command.

The silence in the room is broken when Matoca continues.

"Now go send me your Wards, then wait for me to send them back as Dark-Ryders." Finished speaking, the lights in the room gradually dimmed until the room went black. Then the doors open. The three lords exit the hall, the doors closing behind them.

Yar walks up close to Draka, making him reach for his sword.

"Wait, I just want to talk."

With his hand still on the hilt of the sword, Draka looks at him. He is not sure if he should trust him or slay him.

With reluctance, Draka replies. "Go ahead, talk, but not too close."

Stepping back a little, Yar says in a low voice, "Look, I know we do not get along, but for the sake of finding out what Matoca is up to, let us put away our battle for now and work together. Once we have found out what is on his mind, we can deal with it."

Draka's head jerks toward Scarra, who seems to be unaware of them.

Yar continues. "Let us not bring her in on this now. She is too loyal to Matoca. When the duration is right and we have more information, then I will talk to her."

Everyone knew that Matoca and Scarra were flames. However, to listen to them one would not believe they are. Matoca knows Scarra would not let any harm come to him. So, he uses this to his advantage.

Scarra feels the same way except, she feels that on the turn of her slaying, it would be by his hands. She holds secrets deep in her heart. These, she is unable to speak of, but before that duration comes, she hopes she will have the bravery to speak her heart's desire.

Draka, knowing how he feels about Matoca, makes him unwilling to work with some beings like Yar, whom he would like to be at the end of his sword. It makes him very uneasy. However, he knows if anyone can find out what Matoca is really up to, Yar can; so Draka nods in agreement.

A deceptive grin plays on Yar's lips. *'This is good. When we find out what he is up to, we can slay Matoca. Then, my newly found companion, I will slay you as well.'*

The thought rests in Yar's mind as the two of them walk out of the Kazar. Without another word, they all move toward their Zaruses. They mount and ride their separate ways.

Below, three Zaruses vanish in the darkness. In one of the high towers, two figures watch from a window.

"Do they suspect anything?" The first figure asks, motioning to the three disappearing figures.

"No, they were too busy arguing with each other to notice anything."

Pausing, the first figure continues, "'They will turn on you".

"I know... I will worry about that when the duration comes."

"Okay. But I hope you know what you are doing."

"Do not worry. Everything is under my control. Even as we speak, a messenger is on his way to the dwelling of the Dekams, inviting them to my Kazar under a sign of peace to stop the slaying on both sides."

"Do you think the High Council will come?"

"They will come. I have made sure of it."

"One more thing, would you separate my head from my body?"

There is a long pause as one of the figures moves away from the window. After what seems like many cycles, the silence is broken by one word.

"Come."

Still stands at the window. Her eyes flash, then dim. Turning, she retreats.

******

16

IT BEGINS AGAIN

On the next Turn of the Firelight, a messenger quickly makes his way to the throne room. It has been twelve turns of the Firelight since Matoca sent him to deliver a message to the Dekam High Council of Twelve. He rode hard for several turns to get this message into his Liege's hand.

He only rests long enough to change Zaruses and eat in one of the smaller Marluings. The news of his journey's success is wrapped up in the message he carries from the insider. It is very important to his liege.

Upon entering the throne room, he makes his way to the stone dais at the far end of the hall. He gives Matoca full honors.

"My Liege," the messenger starts. "Your message has been delivered; I have returned with one from the insider." At this, the messenger raises a scroll in his hand.

Gracefully, he holds it out to Matoca. The importance of this information is for Matoca's eyes and ears only. He will not take it kindly if the messenger oversteps his boundaries.

"Read it," Matoca commands, gesturing to the messenger. Rising to his feet, the messenger unrolls the scroll and begins to read.

"Greetings, Matoca: I am glad your messenger has arrived, so I may confide in you. All goes well according to your plan. No one suspects anything. After your messenger departs, I shall meet with the High Council to convince them that this truce is for all of our benefit.

I will also urge them that this could be the only opportunity we have to stop the slaying, along with the battling of our Clans. I am confident that by the duration you read this message, we shall be on our way toward you."

Finished reading, the messenger rolls the scroll up and waits for Matoca's response. His wait lasted only a moment.

"Very good," Matoca's eyes shine under his hood. He points at the messenger and continues. "Go now, prepare rooms for our 'guests'. Have Wards meet them when they are at least two Turns of the Firelight away. Report to me at that duration when they are about to enter the Kazar walls."

"Yes, my Liege!" The messenger responds as he performs honors. He turns and exits the hall.

The closing of the great doors fills the room, then silence. A moment later, Matoca rises from the throne and moves to the wall at the back of the hall. On the wall are portraits of the various fauna of Icka as well as some carved statues of the creatures Matoca favors.

He places his hand on one of the statues of the Rookile--a creature that he respects for its tenacity. Casting a simple utterance, a hidden panel opens just to the right of the statue.

"All is working well." He whispers to himself as he disappears into the opening.

******

My clan has no clue what plans Matoca is about to unfold. But when it happens, our lives will change forever, especially when we are AMBUSHED.

TO BE CONTINUED

******

17

CLAN ADEIAN

Matoca (Ma-toe-ka): Leader of the Adeians. Before his slaying, he was the one who got them all together, but for another reason. This reason has to do with his control of the clans. Being unable to take over all the Regions by himself, he calls for the help of his fellow companions, known as the Lords. He persuades them to help him. They are Draka, Yar, and Scarra. The creator of the Dark Ryders.

Draka (Dra-ca): Born an Adeian of the warrior class. He does not want to rule the region like the others. He wants to slay Matoca and Yar, but not Scarra. He does not know why, but he will protect her with his life force. Draka does not need Dunamis Powers and would rather not be around Users. Torian is the name of his Zarus.

Scarra (Scar-ra): An Adeian Adept in the User Class. Her Sire made her a cape as a present for her commencing from passage to Adept. She has no desire to rule anything, and her Dunamis Powers were stronger than Matoca's before he got help. She does not trust Matoca, but she understands him.

Yar (Yar): Wants to take over Matoca's place, he would like to have his powers and use them on Draka. Yar is not to be trusted but he would use everything to get what he wants done. The question is what?

Torian (Tor-re-an): Is Draka's Zarus, and is the name that is passed down to all of his Zaruses.

******

******

18

THINGS TO KNOW

ADEIAN: A Clan that lives in the Marluings. They are of the Inlar class. Adeians are loyal to their Liege; however, if the Liege does not do right by them, their loyalty will change (A-dee-an)

ADEPT: A clan member who is skilled in the art of their craft within the User Class. This only refers to Clan Adeian.

BAN: Known to all Clans as a large or a small group of the same clan

BANDY: To trade with other clans

BIMU: East from Clan Trion meaning--'The Joining of two lands' (By-muu)

BONDSERVANT: A slave--only used in Clan Adeian

CHIZKA': The smaller moon or Turn of the Twin (Chi-zoo-ca)

CHIZU': The bigger moon or Turn of the Twin (Chi-zoo)

CYCLE: Measurement of time--one year

DAY OF BEING: The day the person was born.

DEADLY ADEIANS' GRIP: Dead man's grip. Last stand for the one holding the weapon.

DIMU: West from Clan Ja' Ree meaning--'Where two ends join' (Dy-muu)

DUNAMIS POWER: Mystical Powers within a physical or mental motion, which produces an energetic force of different types, also known as a Dynamic and or Dynamical (Du-na-mas)

DURATION: This is known throughout the Clans as the passage of time

FAUNA: Adeian, meaning places in the Domain of Icka

FE'TANG: A weapon used by the Adeians in their art of Inlar (Fe-tang)

FLAME: My love or my lover

FULL HONORS: This is done when honoring someone of a higher rank, by making a fist with both hands, crossing the arms against the chest, then slamming them up against the chest, before kneeling

GARGON: A creature that lives in the wetlands, it walks on all six legs; it has a long tail. Its teeth glow red with every bite, which gives the appearance of being a Dragon (Gar-gon)

HIGH ROCK: Known to all Clans as a Mountain

HONORS: This is done when honoring someone of a higher rank, by making a fist with any hand, and slamming it up against the chest, but there is no need to kneel

HORDE: Known to all Clans as a large member of the Adeian Clan, numbering two hundred thousand

ICKA: One of four Domains from Clan Mosaur (I- ka)

INLAR: Adeian-- meaning the art of taking life or assassin (In-lar)

KAZAR: Adeian-- meaning Castle within the realm.

LENTAR: A huge bird that can take a Dekam adult away with ease. Its wingspan is that of an adult Yohba tree (Len-tar)

LEONINE: A cat-like creature that lives in small groups and follows the food, mostly the Mori (Leo-nine)

LIEGE: Known to the Adeians as the King of the lands

MARLUINGS: Adeian cities, towns, and villages (Mar-lu-ings)

MIGHTY: Massive that of the hind legs of the Mori'

MIU: As is known to all the Clans, West from Clan Ja'Ree meaning 'Where two ends Join' (My-u)

NNI RIVULET: As it is known throughout the Clans, it is a body of water that flows through the Domain of Icka

Q'FARHTI: Forest as known to the Veloians, meaning 'Place of Origin'
(Qu-far-ti)

RIVULET: Known to all Clans as Stream or River (Riv-u-let)

ROOKILE: A creature with scales for skin. It is very mean and attacks in groups. The females are the most dangerous. They will stop at nothing to mate (Roo-kile)

SANA: A snake-like creature with a very deadly bite. Lives in the area of the wetland but can also be found in different areas of Icka (Say-na)

SHIFT: The ability to move from one plane to another plane quickly, Veloian for moving out of time

SIRE: Known to all Clans as Father or Mother

SPAN: Known to all Clans as an hour

TALL: Known to all Clans and used mostly by the young ones, an Adult

TEARS: Known to all Clans as to cry

THE DARK ONE: Known to all the clans as the Devil.

TI'FIN: Measurement in inches, used by all in this world.

TURN(S) OF THE FIRELIGHT: Means Day or Days. This is the name of the sun when it rotates around the planet.

TURNS OF THE TWIN: This means the night when both moons rise.

U'FIN: Measurement in feet as it is used by the inhabitants of this world.

UROTH: South from Clan Arkarian, meaning 'Of Opposing Ends' (U-ro-th)

UTTERANCE: Known to all Clans, meaning spoken word form, but used mainly in Clan Veloian

UTTER: Same as Utterance

WARD (S): Known to all Clans as Guards

VILLEINS: Adeian farmers (Vi-le-ins)

YOHBA: A Tree that grows exactly 12 inches every year, max is 100ft (Yo-ba)

YOHB: Used to describe other things such as distance, length, and measurement.

ZANNELLA: A large Adeian Marluing located towards the Zuroth on the other side of the high rocks, ruled by Sham.

ZARUS: A creature used for riding and carrying things (Zar-us)

ZUROTH: North from Clan Meaning from opposite ends (Zoo-ro-th)

This is the beginning of a series of books about this world and its inhabitants. Join our heroes along with their antagonists on their journey as they uncover the Prophecy. Together, they will find the truth.

******

Look for the next book in the line AMBUSH ~part-one~ and learn how a Clan lives and how they relate to each other.